Forbidden Graces
Book Two: The Sensuous Longing of God

by Carol Bridges

© 2012 Earth Nation Publishing

© 2012 Earth Nation Publishing

ISBN 978-0-945-111-05-4

All rights reserved. No part of this book may be reproduced or utilized in any form or by any means, electronic or mechanical, including photocopying, recording, or by any information storage and retrieval system without permission in writing from the publisher.

Earth Nation Publishing
Nashville, IN 47448 USA

Cover Art: Fabric Quilt by Carol Bridges
www.carolbridgesartquilts.com

Manufactured in the United States of America

Introduction

There will be a Time when all that is conscious of itself will reveal its hidden thoughts to the human beings. All of the realms now existing behind the veil of myth will emerge. For some, this has already happened. This is their story of love for the world.

Dedicated to those who have filled me with love.

Forbidden Graces
Book Two: The Sensuous Longing of God

The Return

When Stefan walked through the gate, it was as if he had always been there. The creek giggled a little shyly like a girl attracted to someone she perceives as beyond her reach. The cardinals chirped a note of acceptance. The stones recognized a listener, like themselves. Green plants began fantacizing about their next spring's blooms, imagining their colors just a little more vivid than they had ever been before.

Inside the welcoming house, there was a deep peace in which everything rested, not asleep, but like a cat, completely relaxed yet somehow alert to the slightest movement. The voice of the woman who lives here brings the entire spirit of the house to quiet attention. Recently, there had been a very slight change in the timbre of that voice, a new note of deeper satisfaction. And the other voice, the one flowing into her from Stefan, held the same message.

In the kitchen, the two humans were touching everything as if they were preparing a sacrament of communion. New thoughts were stirring. They knew they were on the threshold of a very important moment.

Sitting across the table from each other now, after the customary compliments and "thank you"'s for the food they were sharing, they paused. Tasting. Their eyes met and their souls slipped into the shining black pool of eternity. Without words, the consciousness of Stefan opened into the consciousness of this woman called Grandmother, and he saw her as a young gypsy woman.

She was walking briskly away from the campfire where the wagon caravans had circled. "Tsura," he heard himself call out. Then, to Stefan, Grandpapa said, "Let her go. Women must think they are free. Pursue her only in your mind by following her with intense thoughts of love. Do not let up. She will return."

After this moment of revelation, Stefan and Grandmother looked with fresh eyes at each other. They could feel the bond of the gypsy travelers still strong within them.

Stefan said, "May I call you Tsura?"

"Yes," said Grandmother. "It will strengthen this part of us now. We are drawing people together again. It is a new life, but we have ancient roots. Our painted wagons are still in our hearts, and we will see them in some form again as we gather on the Hill."

They spoke then of other things, the temple, the river Shemaya, the people who had gathered there that day and, here and there, a question about each other's current lives. A bit of history to ground themselves in each other's Earth presence. The kitchen and the whole house listened and passed the stories on to the garden which quietly informed all the other beings living on the land, all without words.

Instantly, the Hill had the feeling that a clan of conscious beings was returning. Another story in Time was about to be created.

Wren's View

The season was cooling. Leaves shivered a little in the breeze. Bouquets of reds and yellows appeared in the hillside montage. At home in his office, Grandmother's friend, Wren, contemplated how the land around the planned Temple building could be utilized to take advantage of the river view while inviting visitors toward the Temple itself. The walkway from the parking area needed to entice the visitor slowly along a meandering path with places to stop, breathe, contemplate, and then direct their attention to a particular focal point.

There must be areas in which it is easy to feel alone with nature as well as areas which encourage social contact. He went through his files of benches, fountains, statuary, pavement options, plantings and lighting, trying out various arrangements in his mind and sketching possibilities. Once an arrangement felt right, he would go to the Hill, walk the imaginary new path, envisioning his ideas. If they still felt right to him, he would present them to the spirit of the place and to all the realms of living creatures there.

Often, when attuning to the living beings, he would find himself imitating their movements and realize that his design must exhibit similar movement or form. A weeping willow prompted a curved bench that would comfort a lone person while she grieved and gathered strength. A tall pine branching out over the cliff asked for a large, steady rock so that anyone encountering the edge would feel safe, solid and grounded, but also perceive new vistas of potential.

Wren sat gazing out the window and thinking until Shae walked into the studio. "As I think about this landscape of gentle curves and flowing rivers and how deeply it calls to me, Shae, I am reminded of our dance of surrender the night we met. Now, I am learning to surrender to the dance of the land. Whenever I am at the Hill, I am captivated by the light and movement of something there, and I begin to let my body feel its response. This always moves me."

"You are so much at one with the natural energy of a place and connected to its subtleties, Wren. I feel this especially when you respond to me. It seems that every time we make love our talents combine in new ways giving us fresh ideas or new approaches to things that seemed like problems.

"I am still captivated by you, Shae. I had never thought of myself as a dancer, but you taught me that it is not about learning steps but about letting the body speak its own language of movement in tune with the sound. The land and the Temple must dance together as we do. Let me show you my latest landscape drawings and tell you my thoughts on them. Then, would you like to dance this through with me?"

"Of course, give me a few minutes to prepare the space." Shae went to the small meditation room they had created upstairs off the bedroom. It was uncluttered. Thick violet carpet on the floor. Filmy white curtains over the window, softening the light. Large pillows with intricate gold threadwork were stacked in the corner. She lit seven candles, burned sage and sweetgrass to purify the air of prior intentions, brought in a pitcher of water and two goblets to refresh their palettes and placed them on the handcrafted maple table, all actions to let their bodies know it is time to shift their focus to the transcendent.

Wren chose a music selection that spoke to his soul about the feeling he hoped to generate for the Temple landscape. He then showed his plans to Shae as they relaxed on the pillows. After he had spoken and shown her his sketches, they sat face-to-face, and began to call in the God-energy always ready and available. They breathed this blessing into themselves and out through their solar plexus chakras into each other, visualizing the energy as brilliant yellow light, and seeing it penetrate and blend with the yellow light of the other.

After a few minutes of concentration and clarification of their intention, their minds were lifted. They spoke their prayer, opening themselves to the highest vision for their part in the Temple project. Then, they surrendered to the movements which came to them, feeling themselves to be the trees and waters and rolling hills, imagining the scenes and allowing new insights and awareness to rise up within them. Their concentration sent ripples through time and space to all who would eventually cooperate in creating the Temple of Love.

Jampa's Response

Monk Jampa noticed the stream of brilliant yellow light rising up to his personal sanctuary in the Great Land, a place of a higher-frequency vibrational field than Earth, and, therefore, invisible to most humans. Jampa felt the sincerity and gratitude which came from Wren and Shae before any request for assistance. The two senders were truly trying to find the best solutions for the Temple of Love landscape on Earth. The were searching for ways to enhance visitors' experiences and ways to restore and maintain the original harmony of the entire Hill and all its inhabitants since it had been logged years before.

Jampa guided them first to a few books that would provide slightly different perceptions on design possibilities. They both enjoyed reading, and this would give their analytical side something to think about while he took them on a spiritual tour. When they went to the Hill, he would prompt them to, step-by-step, explain a segment of the plan to the area where it would take place, actually speaking to the land itself. Then, he would instruct them to become silent and observe the immediate response of nature.

"If the birds sing sweetly, the deer come into view or the trees rustle softly, there is approval, and all will go well. If a heavy branch falls, the wind gives an uncomfortable blow, or a creature stings or calls out a screech, there is disapproval. If this happens, then, using a dowsing tool, you must question to find the problem and the solution."

Jampa sent these messages into their hearts and gestured to his doves to bring a great helping of his love to surround the two who were beseeching his assistance. Then, he went back to his meditation.

The Music of Children

Monk Kalden had been working alongside Hartford, the main architect of the temple project, as they paced between piano and desk. "I like to keep both sides of my brain open," he told Kalden, "whenever I have an intense design project. The music takes me to another space entirely, and I am swept into a land of all possibilities."

Kalden wholeheartedly agreed. He often attended both heavenly and earthly concerts himself and felt that architecture and music had much in common, the structure of the building needing all of its components to create a visual melody. He encouraged Hartford to review some of his favorite architectural sites and ask himself what musical piece each one was exemplifying.

He also explained how Hartford's love for Nola and the children was providing him with an entire new songbook of possibilities. "You are refreshing your mind on the needs of the young ones, updating your ideas to match the needs of the Time. All of this will facilitate your sensitively creating just the right space for children to be nourished by nature and spirit at the Temple site," said Kalden.

Just then, all three sons came running through the front door, talking excitedly about getting to help Nola build a cob oven in the back yard. She wanted to see if the wood fire-heated clay structure would improve her bread's flavor. Her friends and Farmer's Market customers were already pleased with her wares, but she was always looking for ways to make something even more special.

The boys would love working with the muddy clay and Carlos already was showing considerable artistic skill. He could develop the design. Aron and Dayo would be happy just to build and mold the mud and dream of their first pizza from the outdoor oven they will have constructed themselves. Hartford agreed with all of their ideas and encouraged them to come up with a doable design, taking into account the structural limitations of the clay, sand and straw mix.

The boys scrambled upstairs to the pencils, papers, cob oven-building books and modeling clay. Hartford and Kalden smiled as the idea for the children's area of the Temple of Love began to take shape.

They continued their work to provide a plan for a physical temple structure which would feel as alive as the spiritual Temple of Love in their hearts. Drawing from lives past in which many of Hartford's skills were refined and from Kalden's guidance relating how things are done in the Great Land beyond Earth's present frequency range, they knew they would come up with a design that brought young and old closer to the Spirit Within All Life.

All of the sacred places which had been built throughout the history of Earth had been built on energetically charged ground and structured according to sacred geometry utilizing the finest materials and craftspeople of the time. This was to be no exception.

A Good Place

Molly the dog had been listening to the boys describe their project and had heard many of the conversations between Hartford, Nola and the others who came to talk over the temple plans. She, being an elder and a practical soul wondered if anyone had thought of a burial place on the temple grounds. She was about ready to let this life go, "getting a bit slow," she thought.

Lately, she had begun reviewing her life, the elder boys, Hartford's children, having been tiny toddlers when she arrived that Christmas long ago. She had been hugged, petted, dropped, pushed, pulled, put in toy trucks, run behind bicycles, accompanied them to school, and had wonderful treats nearly every day. Now, with the new family, three lively boys, she wanted to do it all again, but she just did not have the legs for it anymore.

She guessed it had been a darn good life, but she had not compared it to too many others. All the dogs in the neighborhood seemed fairly well off. She had her favorites, of course, but for the most part, she liked home...just to lie on the braided rug in front of the fireplace feeling the warmth of a houseful of kind people. She figured death would come easily there one day, and then she would rest...well...where?...on the Temple grounds. With that vision, she fell asleep.

About Death

    Molly was not alone in her wondering about death. As Hartford lay next to Nola in the night, he wondered how long he would get to experience this blessing. He had already raised two sons, his wife had died and now he had committed all that was left of his life to Nola and her three sons. He was sure he could provide for their physical well-being. Money was abundant. He was pleased that Nola could pursue her studies and eventually take over his business. He was a provider.

    But life is so much more. He really wanted to live, to go through all the phases again, even the rough parts, though the memory has smoothed those edges. "Perhaps, some of those challenges can be left out this time," he thought. "Time. Must I concern myself with time?" he wondered. "I am 70. She is 45."

    The four monks were often called to the rooms of people thinking about death. It was part of their work to listen and to assist the wonderers in reaching a state of peace. Before it is time for the crossing, they subtly steer the contemplative person to books and people who can answer their basic questions.

    "Why me? Why now? Can I get better? What must I do to heal myself? Is my life complete? Have I fulfilled the promise of my being? Must I surrender? What is it like on the other side? Am I deserving of reward or punishment?"

    "They have so many questions," said Monk Chewa. "I like to get most of these answered as quickly as possible, to explain the basics. Yes, you are welcome in the Great Land. There is no judgment other than self-judgment which happens preceding death. Yes, you will re-unite with loved ones in the ways you choose. No, you will not heal yourself this time. The shedding of your human body will be your healing. Then we can go on."

    "After your gentle teaching, Chewa, I like to begin my reminiscences with them, just reminding them of small but important moments and people they have forgotten. This gives them time to work through emotions long set aside," said Monk

Kunchen.

"Not everyone gives themselves this time though," said Jampa. "There are sudden and violent deaths. With these I am very careful to extend my arms fully and open my heart to maximum capacity so that they fall right into me. I cradle them a long time, eventually explaining what needs to happen to the dense body and how to transfer their full awareness to the subtle body which has always been within them.

"It is rare that the human beings have seen their subtle body, but many have felt it when they exchanged the energy of love with another. I remind them of these moments. Very slowly, they begin to understand. Soon, I have them watching the old body as it is laid to rest and point out that they are no longer in it. When I ask them how they feel at this point, they are always surprised to say, 'Very well, indeed!'"

"Jampa, you are an excellent assistant to these souls. Though I realize there must be completion of the world belief systems of duality before this type of death is no longer needed, my heart always spills a bit from its chalice of love to those who have chosen a sudden or violent death. Perhaps I will never be able to hold steady during such an occasion," said Kalden.

"Your feeling is very natural, Kalden. We all go through this until we stabilize the idea of everlasting life in our consciousness. Just knowing this truth does not keep us from wanting to stop harsh actions. Love always behaves thus. But, our job now is to steady this chalice of love so that it is completely full and can be offered in its completeness to the one who comes so quickly before us. It is these who have died in extreme conditions who need every ounce of this divine nectar," said Chewa.

"Let us go now to those who call us," said Kunchen.

The River's Flow

Streams of silver river Shemaya meander through the brilliant woodlands listening, singing, listening, bringing all the news from all its sources to the wild things living there. Water carries the consciousness of all, carries the light, feeds the living land and all the people. There is nothing outside its touch. "I bring the message that the people have become ready to bring the Temple of Love into form. Their desire for peace and goodwill has finally outpaced their competitive run. Drink from this joy I carry," called the river, "Drink and be merry."

EC began to cry and George grabbed her up for a dance. They ran to the river to fill their jugs. They joined the other Faer Folk and all the animals nearby. "A toast to the humans," they lifted their mugs. "A Temple of Love shall be built!" They knew in their hearts how hard it had been for the humans to release their pain, to forgive the debts and shortcomings that had come from their limited vision. They also knew the strength and courage of the steadfast keepers of the way. It was these who made the temple stones, the etheric structure of compassion. It had hovered near for so many years just waiting for this moment. Like a blueprint drawn upon the sky, it could only be seen with spiritual eyes. So many obstacles had to be overcome.

Now, each day as the river rolled and the creatures followed their paths, each would send a message to all others regarding the proceedings. A tree planted. A set of plans offered for approval or suggestion. Rituals of gratitude. Contemplations. Reflections. Renewals of commitment to the goal.

The Hearth

"I have been thinking of the hearth," said Hartford as he went into the kitchen for a break from his work and a touch of Nola's light. "It was always the heart of the home and the place of nourishment before we became too busy to make this warm, comforting spot the main gathering place in our homes. Ideally, home is the place in which each person is fed not only physically but emotionally, mentally and spiritually as well. It was always a natural activity to gather 'round a fire, eat and talk, until we decided fires were messy and dangerous, eating became a complicated health challenge, and talking was transmitted through plastic and electronic devices. How can souls be nourished without the hearth?

"We once depended on a person to make our fires, cook our food, tell us stories. In the not-too-distant past, these activities were performed by the same person who then became very special because of their fire-building, cooking and storytelling skills. Who warms us now? Who makes that special dish we love? Whose stories reach inside and touch our hearts? Too often, it is no one near, perhaps no one we have ever met, no one we have touched flesh to flesh.

"As humans, we long for this kind of experience. It is the fire, the messy, dangerous events of life that wake us up. We want some human to reveal his or her real heart as we feel each other's warm skin right next to ours. This is what the hearth can encourage. It is not slick, sterile or quick. It does not connect you with business. It is not made to express a popular style. It is simply the place to be nourished in every way.

"Since you and the children have been here, Nola, I feel this primal fulfillment once again. You bless my life each day, not only by your presence, but by keeping all the home fires burning ... love, bread and passion."

"I have learned to keep the energy moving through me," responded Nola. "I have released the idea that I am torn between two choices or two experiences or two powers. These thoughts block the flow. I am simply choosing to be a vessel of the God-current, to let myself be filled with the beauty of life around me and to pour it out into others. I feel like a river runs through me."

"Shemaya, the river of listening and delivering the divine message. Yes. This river of love carries me through each day and one day will carry me beyond this life. I realize as I contemplate my own death, that that which can be taken away by death is truly unimportant. It is the full expression of the heart which cannot be taken. That is what is important," Hartford continued. "My energies now are all directed toward this goal, to create the Temple of Love at every level, with you, at home, in my music, in my work, in my interactions with the world."

Nola savored Hartford's words as she always had. She turned the flame down under the soup she had been making as she felt the warmth of her own feelings for this man who sat before her. She ran her fingers across the butter and put them to his lips, sealing the thinking mind and tantalizing the palette. "What flavors of life would you enjoy today, my wise friend?" she asked.

"Whatever you place before me, I will taste and enjoy," he replied.

The soup bubbled and simmered pleasantly. The butter began to melt. The bread waited without its spread. The wooden spoon wished it had a fork. The towel slipped to the floor. The kitchen chair scooted to the side. The refrigerator hummed as if it were paying no attention. Butternut squash and cinnamon scented the air. Everything in the whole kitchen began to feel just a little bit closer.

The Spot

Stefan, having only recently moved to town, had not yet made friends with his rented room. He had not been there long and did not plan to stay. He had come to town for other reasons, magical, mysterious reasons. He had been guided by visions of green hillsides, rain, people coming together in circles of joy, gardens overflowing with fruit and vegetables, small dwellings and the image of a woman holding a rock.

He figured most of the images were simply desires he had to live a simple, Earth-attuned life. But, the woman with the rock was a puzzle. He had just kept these images in the back of his mind and began to research where such a fertile land might be and whether there might also be communal activities going on there. He narrowed his search to five "most-likely" places and checked them out. None called to him strongly until Indiana. When looking at the map, he saw in his mind's eye a remarkable temple hovering over a specific area. Then, he saw the woman's hand holding the stone and placing it as a small part of the temple wall.

"This is the spot," he thought and began immediately to pack up his things. It was a long way from Arizona, but the drive would give him time to contemplate the future and make peace with the past.

Remembering these visions on his way to Tsura's again, he had to smile when he drove past The Spot, Dance and Juice Bar Cafe. "Yes," he thought, "No need to remind me; I know I am here where I belong."

Tsura was waiting at the door of her house, having felt his presence coming closer and closer. "It has been so long since I have danced, Stefan, and my friend Ayotunde is playing tonight at The Spot. Would you like to go?"

"Yes, I just passed the place and felt it was a confirmation that I have reached my destination. Now, you are solidifying that idea. Ever since I offered my life to the Spirit, I have been guided to the most amazing experiences. Meeting you, of course, tops my list."

On the way to town they spoke of coincidences, signs and synchronicities and how such things had affected their lives, each story connecting their hearts even more strongly.

"Here we are, Tsura. May I have this dance?"

Inside

Shae, Wren and Keara were at a table near the stage. The owners, being dancers themselves, cleared plenty of space for those who enjoyed wildly dancing. Tables were pushed back. The wooden floor was highly polished. Fresh juice bar. Live food. Live music. Great musicians. Ayotunde!

You could not continue sitting very long. Bodies filled the space with excitement, a fireworks display of people sparkling, touching, twirling. Shoes came off. Excess clothing was tossed on chairs. Long hair flew. Eyes closed. Trance dancing. Forgetting everything else. Only being. Only moving. All of the self given to life.

They danced until closing. Feeling so good. Sweat. Sweet. Sensuous. "Come home with me, Stefan. Spend the night."

"There is nothing I would like more." Dreamy, perfect ride home. Feeling close. Feeling empty of everything but the present. Feeling the movement of this dance, the dance of pairing, of finding, of knowing. How magical life is!

Deeper Inside

"I want nothing from you, Stefan, but I am open to whatever you offer me."
"I feel the same, Tsura. I am simply a servant of the Great Grace which flows through us. I have no other agenda."
"Then let us go to bed, naked in body and soul. We shall see what comes of it as our senses and our spirits work out the details."

Humans are comforted by cloth. It provides a measure of protection. It keeps us warm or cool. It gives us a sense of style or of belonging to a certain group. It can give, or take away, status. Removing layers of cloth, we give up these surface pieces of our ego, getting down to the unchangeable or, at least, to the what-I-am-now portion of ourselves.

Often, we slip in-between other coverings, the bedsheets and blankets. Their feel also describes us in some way. Will we lie down in beds of satin and silks or upon green grasses or fields of hay? Just as we find comfort in certain textures of cloth for our bed to feel just right, it also takes many layers of revealing ourselves to each other to bring us comfort in sleeping with another. Many layers of energy merge to bring us toward closeness or coldness, unity or isolation.

For Tsura and Stefan now, after sharing their souls, to remove the layers of cloth which separated their bodies was as easy as folding back the blanket, putting the project aside and just enjoying the accomplishment of the work thus far, a thing artists do. Everything created with the touch of human hands is a work of art. Quality may vary, but it is still a work of art.

Stefan, as a sculptor of clay and stone, was adept at recognizing an especially sensuous curve, or line, or play of light. Every motion gave the form a fresh perspective he could appreciate. Tsura, enjoyed the feel of things - cloth, earth, bodies - each sensation feeding her as much as food. There was no hiding the true self, no desire to hold back the river of love that was flowing between them. They wrapped each other in the rainbow light of their pure intention to offer the very highest energies to each other and drifted into sleep.

Dreaming Down

From the Great Land, Tha and Grandmother watched their Earth selves, Stefan and Tsura. "One more life together, Tha. I think this one will be quite interesting. I wonder how they will handle their age differences."

"They may not notice them. They are sense-adepts after all. And we are their High Selves. They will continue where we left off in terms of building the Temple of Love on Earth. We have but to keep them supplied with the etheric building blocks. We now work without limitation and can free them of many burdens they thought they may have to carry unto death."

"But, Tha, you did carry them to death, did you not?" questioned Grandmother.

"Only the burdened physical body has been laid to rest. We are their True Beings. Do you not recall seeing me regain my youthful appearance as soon as my spirit ascended? I dissolved all the stress and strain of my Earth body immediately at death. Then, I had two years by Earth time to restructure my life here."

"Did I die, Tha?"

"In a manner of speaking. That day on the Hill when you were resting, feeling that your work was finally going to be accomplished, I pulled you up to be with me and our Divine Family. Together, we decided to allow you to go on for you held such wisdom regarding the project. But, we also wanted to share our lives physically again as the Golden Age came into being, therefore, I chose to return with you, this time as Stefan.

"You were given a new wave of vitality. So, you see, Stefan and Tsura may not be aware of their age differences. We have activated the memory of their gypsy lives in them, for these memories will guide the next portion of their decisions regarding the people working on the Temple of Love. You are, therefore, alive and well, as am I. We share this new dream of ourselves as the Temple of Love becomes manifest on Earth."

"Wow, Tha, I can't wait to experience our whole story."

Grandmother and Tha laughed and strolled together to the Library of Memories so that they could further inspire themselves on Earth in their new life as Stefan and Tsura. Their path meandered through woodland glades, turning at just the right moments to give them views of the cosmic river and the falls of light.

Earth Dawn

Awakening in her physical Earth body, Grandmother Tsura exclaimed, "Oh my, Stefan," I feel as though I have been completely cleansed in a great shower of light. Your body is such a powerful transmitter!"

"Mmmmm...really?" Stefan mumbled as he woke up. "Enjoy. And hold me close. Enjoy."

Pink sky turned clear blue as the birds readied their nests for winter. The trees continued their annual housekeeping chores, tossing old leaves every which way. Stripping down. Bringing their expansive nature back down to their roots. Storing food supplies. The squirrels checked on their stash of nuts, always wanting just a few more. Just in case.

Back in the Little People's village, EC shook out her rugs. George polished his tools. They considered taking a slight vacation while all the animals had plenty of food supply on hand, but couldn't think of anywhere else they would rather be.

It was going to be a good winter.

Child Sight

Through all the seasons of their twelve years of life, Nimi and Bryn came to the Hill together. Nimi felt the frailty of Bryn's physical being as well as the strength of his spirit. They would go to the cliff side where the portal to the Higher Realms had opened. There, they would lie on the ground or just sit hoping it would open for them.

They found that if they were very quiet, paying attention to all of the subtle sounds around them, soon they would feel a floating sensation and imagine themselves flying out over the glen below. Sometimes, they would just enjoy the flight and return. But, today was different.

"Nimi, I see a huge building. This must be the Temple everyone has spoken of. Do you see it?"

"Yes, let's go in. Can you find the door?"

"It is over here. I can't seem to push it open."

"Wait Bryn, we must ask permission and state our intention, remember?"

"Yes. I am Bryn. This is my friend, Nimi. We are kind. We would like to enter and find out more about you. Our parents and friends are trying to build you on the Hill and, perhaps, we can help them. May we come in?"

The huge door swung open by itself, light pouring out toward them so that they could not initially see what was inside. But, they took a step, paused, then another step, paused, then another. The floor was reading their energy.

Having deemed it compatible, the light dimmed enough for them to see. Huge blocks of stones were stacked, or so it appeared, creating giant walls that soared to a height they could not perceive.

They walked gently over to the first section of stone wall. Touching the stone, it came alive, almost like a television screen. Inside the stone, there seemed to be a living movie taking place. They sat down to watch.

In one of the stones, they saw lines of hungry people with

empty bowls. The people looked sad and hopeful at the same time. At the front of the line, there were people filling the bowls and saying cheerful words. The lines seemed endlessly long, so Bryn suggested they move on to another stone.

Nimi looked around, not wanting to just go down the line. Perhaps there were more interesting stories being told. Though the stones at first appeared to be white, as she looked closer, there seemed to be slight hues of color to each one. She said, "Let's try pink, this one over here."

Bryn followed and they touched the pink stone. Again, a screen-like phenomenon took place. This time, they saw a child in a crib. He was crying and his mother was coming to attend to his needs. Bryn recognized Saffi, his mother; then, he saw that he was the child.

"That's you, Bryn!" said Nimi.

The mother, Saffi, picked up Bryn, the child, and held him snuggly in her arms. She spoke of how she and Yaro had waited a long time before inviting him into their lives, wanting to be able to provide a safe home in a world which appeared quite unsteady at the time. She talked about their dreams of living in a community of helpful people who cared for each other and were committed to creating a peaceful life. The baby was soothed by her words. Then she began to sing.

Bryn began to cry a little. "Nimi, I am going to have to leave Saffi and Yaro soon. They do not know this. I don't want them to be saddened, but I am needed elsewhere. You must help me. How can I do this properly?"

"Oh, Bryn, will you please come back through this portal from time to time or may we visit you here? I will miss you so much."

"I don't yet know. We must find Jampa and ask him. I only know that I have promised to assist the world in its transformation by helping as many people as I can before the energetic shift takes place. Saffi and Yaro needed to feel the completion of having a child they could care for properly and to whom they could offer the life they had been working so hard to create. This wish has been fulfilled.

"I know they would like to provide this for a long time into the future, but I have also promised other souls that I will be born to them. I am especially skilled at taking on physical or mental conditions that call forth extreme loving action from my caretakers. This is a great gift to their souls. Can you help everyone to understand this?"

"I will do my very best, Bryn. Perhaps we should go home now and think about these things. We can summon Jampa tonight in our prayers and get his advice as well. I love you so much, Bryn."

They hugged with the innocence of childhood and the wisdom of a thousand lives. They were not ready to read other stones that day and again passed through the giant door of the Temple of Love and floated back down to the Hill into their physical bodies. Jampa was standing invisibly at the edge of the woods, as always, keeping an eye on the course of the young ones' lives. He would wait undiscovered until they called him with their evening prayers.

Evening Prayers

Kate-Amee noticed that when Nimi came home from the Hill, she seemed a bit disturbed. "Everything alright, Nimi?" she asked.

"I have a mission, Mama, but I cannot talk about it right now. I have to do some writing and thinking," replied Nimi.

"Okay, but remember that we are all here to help you if you need help of any kind," said Kate-Amee.

Nimi went to her room, closed the door and got out her handmade journal. She began chronicling the events of the day, a practice she often did when special things happened or when she was a bit confused about the course life seemed to be taking. Just writing things down always helped her to gain a bit more clarity. Then, she would know the right questions to ask Jampa whom she trusted as her personal spiritual advisor.

She liked those words, "personal spiritual advisor." They made her feel as though her questions were as important as those of the President or the Pope or a famous movie star. "Gosh, I hate to lose my friend, Bryn," she thought. "Could he not help people on Earth without being born into their families?" she wondered. He did seem, as he said, good at having a handicap of some kind, but would he always have to have a handicap?"

She tried to think of other things because it was not yet bedtime and she figured Jampa was not ready to hear her prayers at 3pm in the afternoon unless there was an emergency. She decided to go to the garden and see if Papa needed help.

"Can I help, Papa?" she asked as she found Reuban in the garden.

"Of course, Nimi. Get the rake and begin raking all the leaves into a pile by the compost bin. That would be a great help to me. How are you doing today?"

"I have a mission, but I cannot talk about it yet. Perhaps tomorrow. Today, I have to think," Nimi replied.

Reuban was used to Nimi's need for private time. She was a deep thinker, very serious about life and very spiritually aware. Mirela and Nickolas, thus far, seemed mainly concerned with their own lives and the fun that could be had in the moment, but Nimi thought in cosmic terms. Reuban very much enjoyed her ideas and questions.

"What do you think the trees are feeling today as they drop their leaves?" he asked Nimi, just to get her mind on the moment and see if she would like to explore the greater significance of this change of seasons.

"I think they are sad, a little bit, because they have cared about these leaves all summer and now the leaves are leaving them. They must know that they will return next spring, but I don't think they can help but feel some sense of loss right now." Then she began to cry.

"Tell me, Nimi, if you want to talk about it now," Reuban said as he went to her with an offer of his father arms.

Nimi fell into them and sobbed while Reuban quietly waited for her to be ready to speak words that might explain what was going on inside her. "You can't tell anyone yet, Papa, but Bryn is going to die soon. He is going to leave us because he has to help other people, different families."

"How do you know this, Nimi?"

"On the Hill, we went into a place in the sky where the Temple is waiting and we saw a picture of him, a moving picture of him when he was a baby. Saffi was telling him how much they wanted him and loved him. Then he told me that he had fulfilled his time with Saffi and Yaro and other people needed him to be born into their families. I will miss him so much, Papa."

They remained silent for awhile in each other's arms. "Nimi, I think we all need to think about this for awhile. Is this the mission you were referring to? Are you thinking you might leave us as well?"

"No, Papa, I don't think so. My mission is to ask Jampa

how to help Saffi and Yaro when Bryn goes away."

"That is a large burden for just one little girl, Nimi. I think Jampa may agree that more of us should be involved in this. But, I promise not to say anything until we have all thought about this overnight. I will ask my Guides as well. This will be very difficult for Yaro and Saffi, but with all of us helping them through it, I know things will turn out right. Let us just take a minute to thank the trees for bringing this subject to our attention. They love us so much."

"Trees," said Nimi, "Thank you."

"Trees," said Reuban, "Thank you for showing us how to gracefully bow to the cycles of life. We continue to be open to your wisdom. Amen."

Nimi's Room

When Nimi went upstairs to her room, Jampa was already waiting for her, sitting in her desk chair by the window. "Nimi, I thought that perhaps you would like me to come early. I was sensitive to your tears. I felt them from far away and came quickly. It seems the trees and Reuban had everything in hand, however, so I just waited here to see what you had to share with me today."

Nimi explained the situation to Jampa and explored her feelings of loss and what might be done with them. Jampa listened carefully and very patiently until she had poured everything out that her soul was holding on the matter.

"What comes to you now, Nimi?" asked Jampa. "Now that you are empty? Pause just a minute and see what ideas come into your mind."

"I think maybe Mama should talk to Saffi because they are friends. Maybe Papa should talk to Yaro. Maybe we should all meet with Grandmother. I think that Bryn should tell them what he has told me. Then, we will all be present to hold the truth and feel what needs to be done."

"Very wise, Nimi, very wise," said Jampa. "Here is my suggestion. You can explain things to Reuban and Kate-Amee, the whole plan. Then, suggest that they call Saffi and Yaro and arrange a meeting at Grandmother's because Bryn has some important things to discuss with everyone. Of course, you need first to tell this plan to Bryn and get his approval. After the meeting is set, talk to Grandmother and let her know, without telling the details, that Bryn needs to talk about an important matter which will require the help of all invited. I will make my rounds and let the other monks know the situation. We will all bring relevant pieces of information to each person so that their consciousness is as prepared as can be for the news of Bryn's ascension. How does that sound to you?"

"Oh, Jampa, I knew you would help me. Thank you so much. I am going to tell Papa right now, so that he does not have to worry all evening. I love you, Jampa."

"And I love you, Nimi."

    The room felt a bit sad when Jampa and Nimi left. It had so many memories of Nimi and Bryn talking and playing together. The curtains wished a good wind would come in the window and blow off a little of the tension they were experiencing, but the window was closed. The journal lay open on the desk, hoping for a more uplifting piece of news sometime in the next few pages. The calendar wondered which day would be chosen for Bryn's leaving and sort of wished that it could erase that number from its face. The bedroom door closed very quietly, not wanting to disturb any of these thoughts for they were all proper and very natural. It placed its consciousness, however, on the hall side of the door and left the room alone. It would then be able to be the harbinger of the next piece of news.

Sunset

Nimi ran to the garden looking much brighter than she had before. She told Reuban of Jampa's visit and their plans. Reuban said that he would speak with Kate-Amee after the other children were in bed and Nimi could join them if she wished or just leave it up to him to relay the messages. He suggested that they not bring it up at dinner, and that maybe some especially comforting food might accompany dinner and asked Nimi if she might prepare something.

"Yes, Papa, I think hot chocolate would be good. It is almost dinner time and I don't have time to make something complicated."

"Fine. A good choice," said Reuban. "Now, let me finish these chores before I come in. Go help Mama in the kitchen."

The sun was turning orange over the fields. Birds were singing their evening song. Reuban himself now felt the sadness as he put away the rakes and baskets. How hard it would be, he thought, to lose one of his own children or Kate-Amee. Nearly unbearable pain pierced his heart for just a moment before he grabbed that arrow and broke it in two. "No," he said to himself. "I know there will be grief, but I do not have to add to it, just realize that this is the pain that Saffi and Yaro will carry for awhile and love them through it."

Kate-Amee was smiling at the window, "Look at the beautiful sunset, Nimi."

"Yes, Mama," Nimi said without looking. She got out the cocoa and the milk saying, "We need to celebrate the sunset with hot chocolate today."

"Okay," said Kate-Amee suspecting that something was up, but being willing to wait to be told. "There is a time for everything, and it is best to wait for that right moment," she thought. "Everything works so much better that way."

Night Talk

All of the children asleep. The wood fire burning steadily in the stove. Doors closed snugly. Reuban and Kate-Amee holding each other to feel the physical warmth as well as the emotional warmth of each other's presence. "Tell me," Kate-Amee begins. Waits.

Reuban retells the story of Bryn and Nimi at the Hill, Nimi and Jampa's plan, and asks for Kate-Amee's response.

"Oh, this will be so hard for Saffi and Yaro,"

"How can we help them, Kate-Amee?"

They both waited for their insides to stop churning, for the possible scenarios to settle down, for the deep knowing to come. They talked over memories of all their times with Saffi and Yaro, the friendships shared, the fun, the starting of the school, watching the children grow, solving their problems, planning their lives, trying to make a strong foundation for their futures.

"Futures," said Kate-Amee. "It can't be about 'futures,' can it? We focus on the present as much as possible, but it seems we cannot help also visualizing a future arising out of it. Isn't this natural, Reuban? Aren't we designed this way, to always project into the future? At least somewhat?"

"Yes, but we must also be open to many 'futures,' many possibilities. Our minds are so often limiting what can be by remembering past experiences and projecting them forward. There must be something good that can come of this even though, at this moment, I don't have a clue as to what that might be," said Reuban.

Their minds searched for ways to shield their friends from a terrible grief, for reasons why life worked this way sometimes, for assurances that this could be worked through, for anything that would comfort, that would get everyone across this bridge over the abyss. Prayers. Sleep. Trust in the process.

Bryn's Journey

The moon nearly full now, watching over the forest below, touching the heart of the young man alone in his room. Soft light. Guiding One standing near, boat ready for the journey to the Great Land. Jampa comes to the bedside of Bryn.

"Jampa, I know I must go soon, but I am a bit afraid. I like it here and have many friends who will miss me, and I will miss them. My parents will be very sad. Will you help me please?"

"Of course, Bryn, this is why I have come. Nimi, Reuban and Kate-Amee are planning to be with you at Grandmother's house if you should choose to talk to them all about your leaving. Or, you may leave with us tonight, if you wish. There are many strong souls who will work together to assist everyone who will mourn your loss. The choice is yours."

"They may try to convince me to stay if I tell them ahead of time, Jampa. And I will be persuaded by the strength of their emotions. I know now that the bird I saw on the Hill is the phoenix, a mythical bird which rises from the ashes transformed. And three boys on horses who also had great wings called to me to come with them that day. I would have gone, but my family and friends here called me back. I felt their love and need of me so strongly, I returned."

"Yes," said Jampa, "We understand this. This is why we have come to you this evening. Would you like a few hours to say good-bye?"

"Yes, Jampa, I would."

Bryn looked around his room, remembering so many things that happened there. He listened for the sounds emanating from the rest of the house. He felt his comforter lying over him in bed, the feel of his own physical body, the feel of his decision.

Then he got up and went downstairs. Saffi was reading. Yaro was in the kitchen putting some dishes in the cupboard. Bryn said, "Dad, come outside for just a minute, will you?" Bryn thought that maybe the darkness would hide his tears.

"Sure, Bryn, just a minute." Outside, Bryn pointed out the nearly full moon and asked, "Would you still love me if I were on the moon, like an astronaut or something?"

"Of course, Bryn. Are you thinking of becoming an astronaut?"

"Maybe. I am thinking I will have to leave home someday. Not that I want to, but because I have to go to work, kind of like you do. But, I might have a job that is far away, and I won't get to come home every night."

"I suppose that is the way of things. Children grow up, leave home, go off to work or to have adventures somewhere far away."

"That's it, Dad. I have to go on a far away adventure; but it is also work."

There was a long pause as Yaro figured out the message Bryn was trying to convey. "Bryn, I love you so very, very much. You know I will always be thinking of you no matter where you are, no matter what you do. No matter what work you choose. I will miss you terribly, of course. That is natural for fathers, at least this father.

"Your mom and I have known that you could leave your physical body at any time. We have not wished to dwell on this, but to live the moments we do have to share, to live them fully and with appreciation of the gifts that we are to each other. It has been so good, Bryn. I trust that it will continue to be good for all of us.

"Remember that we have all learned to reach the Great Land in our meditations and are learning now to perceive the High Beings with our physical eyes as our bodies adjust to the new energy taking place on the planet. These skills take time to develop, of course, so we may not be as quick as we would like at achieving our goals in this regard. But, you know that we are trying and will continue to do so, so that we may see you in your Higher Self."

"Dad, I don't know for sure how things work there, but I know I have to help some other people who are still on Earth by becoming part of their family. I may not be available right away to visit with you and mom. But, I will ask Jampa to teach me how to communicate with you. And I will appear or call or write letters or find some way to do so. I know there must be a way. There is a way."

"There is a way, most definitely." Yaro hugged Bryn, the hug of utmost caring, the hug of thankfulness, the hug of sorrow, the hug of good-bye, the hug of the eternal journey of every person who has ever loved."

Together, they walked into the house and strode confidently like men, like very strong and spiritual men, over to Saffi. They just stood there in their god-forms being present, being fully present.
She knew then.

Her tears could not help but flow profusely. Woman tears. Love tears. Heartbreak tears. Deep, deep sorrow tears. Release tears. Family tears. Unbearable tears. Accepting tears. And finally, tears of appreciation for all that they had shared together.
They walked together to Bryn's room. "May we lie here with you, Bryn, if we do not interfere?" Saffi asked. Bryn looked for Jampa who was standing nearby. Jampa nodded.
"Yes. Sing me a song as I go to sleep. I will remember it forever. After I am asleep, then go to your rooms please, and don't come back until morning. This is how it must be."
"So be it, Bryn." Saffi then began to sing, as many songs as she could remember ever singing to Bryn. After awhile, Yaro also began to sing with her even though he did not know the words very well. Soon, his own words came flowing out, a song of prayer, a song of journeying, a sailor's song for the sea of consciousness.
Bryn held their hands until he fell asleep. They kept

singing until they were certain he was gone.

Sailor's Voyage

"Don't look back right now, Bryn," said the Guiding One. "Soon enough you will be able to travel back and forth without worry, but right now the waters are a little rough and we must attend to the ship. Take hold of the oars here and head for that distant light."

Jampa was right there as well, adding his strength to the movement. Bryn had seen many movies of dangerous sea voyages, and they were excellent at holding his focus. The wizards of the Great Land had no trouble at all creating whatever special effects were necessary for the facilitation of consciousness shifts. They could make a mighty storm if needed or settle into a calm lagoon. Often, it took a variety of experiences to get one fully across.

"What about my..." yelled Bryn as the storm began to rage.

"Never mind that now, mate," said the Guide. "We have to get through this storm. Look at those waves ahead!"

For many hours, or was it days, or merely moments, the journey continued, keeping Bryn focused on the light ahead. Meanwhile, his body rested peacefully on his bed and the sweet voices of his mother and father entered every cell of his body, there to wait until Bryn would be able to recover the cellular memories stored there for his review.

The hard rain pouring down on the heavenly traveler blended with the voices until a new song was created, a song of things ahead, a song of welcome, a song of life continuing. Such magicians these wizards were. So brilliant the plan of the Great Being.

Now, the storm subsiding, the boat drifted into colorful mists with leaping dolphins and land in sight.

"Look ahead, Bryn, look ahead," said Jampa. And Bryn began to see.

Friendship

The morning call from Reuban was answered by Yaro. "Yes, he is gone," said Yaro. "Please come over with Grandmother."

Kate-Amee, Reuban, Nola and Grandmother arrived with soothing teas and sweet breads and all of their ceremonial objects. Grandmother had been working on a quilt for Bryn for a long time, knowing as she did that he would be passing on in young life. This would wrap the body. Kate-Amee had prepared a special oil with which to anoint the body. Reuban and Yaro removed unnecessary things from Bryn's room in order to make room for others who would be summoned to come.

All in Grandmother's Circle were called. Arriving, each one immediately took responsibility for whatever needed to be done in that moment. Hartford had just completed taking care of the paperwork involved in creating a cemetery area on the Hill for members of their church, the legal definition of their Temple. Stefan and Andret went to dig the grave along with Nimi who would choose the exact location based on her knowledge of Bryn's favorite places. Keara, Ayotunde, Wren and Shae began putting their ideas together to create a proper ritual. Roan was flying in, but would not arrive until after the burial.

The group had thoroughly discussed death and life throughout their Circle times with Grandmother. There was no question about how everything should proceed. Each knew their talent, their skill, their place in the scheme of this event. Each also had great respect for all of the others involved.

The circumstances surrounding death are just as important as those surrounding birth. Each can happen outside of expected timing and one must be ready for all possibilities. Though both birth and death had been delegated in the twentieth century to "professionals," this was no longer acceptable to those whose sensitivities compelled them to make each of these occasions one of true soul expression.

Birth is a death of the life one had been living as a single, independent unit. Death is the birth of such a single, independent unit into a vast unity with All That Is. Neither can be viewed as less important than the other. All feelings around these occasions must be acknowledged: fear, irritation, pain, sorrow, expectation, elation, acceptance.

In many layers of cloth, Bryn's body was wrapped. He was transported by the men as he was himself a man. The women sang and blessed the path with cornmeal, sage and sweetgrass. Circling the grave, they spoke their prayers for Bryn's journey, expressed their love and thankfulness for his presence in their lives and laid their token gifts beside him.

There were soft bells and quiet strings played in the distance as the spirits of nature joined them. Sun shone just right to provide a channel of rays from the heavens. Trees breathed deeply expanding their essence to encompass all. The four monks stood, one in each direction, silently keeping the boundary safe from wandering onlookers. The Guiding One told Bryn, "You may look back now that we are safely at our destination. Look back on those who love you and offer them some knowing in their hearts that you have made the crossing well. Our ship is safe and you are home."

The Dark

The forest was silent for awhile after the people left. Every being respected the gift of the human body the Earth had been given. The four monks, being able to walk between all worlds, took the body down into the deep dark. It was like sinking into the sea, floating down, giving back to the earth all the elements that rightfully belonged to her, all that she had loaned the spirit for this creature who now no longer needed them.

Deep down letting go, the spirit being freed from every molecule of physical life, every bit of heaviness, every fragment of earthly concern. For now it was rest time, just like in the fairy tale of Sleeping Beauty, a long, quiet rest until awakened by the heavenly prince of a new self. First, there must be the kiss of all the sweet good-byes that floated down from above, the gifts of all the mourners' love.

Chewa touched the locket, a golden heart placed on a ribbon around Bryn's neck containing a photograph of the family, Yaro, Saffi and Bryn. Her touch transmitted the feelings contained therein to Bryn's soul in the Great Land. She gathered the other gifts in her large pockets to take to him there where he would contemplate many days on their meaning to him and to the giver. From these gifts and all that was contained within them, he would learn much about the life he had just completed.

Kalden, Kunchen and Jampa very carefully arranged all of the physical energetic elements in a sacred mandala formation as they had done many times with paintings made of colored sand. All of the monks continued their prayers throughout the night, knowing that the design of the mandala along with their prayers would assist all of the humans now adjusting to their loss of young Bryn and help Bryn to adjust to his new level of being.

A young deer wandered over to the gravesite. His mother guided him away. EC brought her little broom of straw bristles and swept the footprints away. George circled the grave with the most beautiful fall leaves he could gather. Juanita placed a small wooden bowl she had shaped nearby so that dew or raindrops might collect there and quench the thirst of the traveling soul. Carl wove a cloth of grass and gently laid it over the grave just to keep it warm on this cool night, not that there was a need to do so, but as a gesture of his fondness for the boy. Bonjockay brought his collection of dried rose petals and placed a few over the place where Bryn's heart might have been. Fred brought a bag of fresh oatmeal cookies flavored with dried cherries and hickory nuts. These he carefully arranged on a tray of sycamore bark and put them by the dew-catching bowl.

    They stayed awhile to make sure their gifts were not disturbed by curious animals until they were certain that the work of the four monks was complete and the soul of Bryn had had the opportunity to view their gifts and know how much they cared for him. Many hours later it would not matter if the animals came along as the clean-up crew, for it was, indeed, their job to keep the forest tidy.

Moonlight

    At home in her room, Nimi looked at the moon now full and decided that it must be Bryn who had joined Grandmother Moon to complete the full circle of light she was now showing. Nimi took her small hand mirror and sat it on the dresser in such a way that it reflected this full moon light, the light of Bryn's soul, and brought it into her room. With this comfort, she climbed into bed and fell into a sound sleep.
    Down the hall, Reuban and Kate-Amee explained to the younger children all of the events of the day and said that they would have a bonfire tomorrow night at which time all those who could not be at the ceremony of burial today could share their prayers and stories of Bryn.

    "I am going to go to the barn now, Kate-Amee, for a little while and be with Cascade. I need to ride."
    "Be careful."
    "I will."

    Reuban climbed atop his huge draft horse, Cascade, and rode out across their pasture. He could not go as far as he wished during the dark of night, but it did not matter. He just felt the need to immerse himself in the night with a creature as powerful as this. Fall is all about death and transformation, letting go and having faith that there will be another spring, another round of life as good as new. The lesson of cycles was everywhere around him and shored up his conviction that Bryn, too, would continue. Life would go on.

Sonata

Hartford sat down at his piano immediately upon returning home. His composition, begun the day Bryn was thought to be lost on the Hill, continued to develop. He played from the passion of grief to the resurrection of life eternal.

Nola lit the wood in the fireplace, turned off the lights, called to Molly who was not far away, and put her feet up on the ottoman. She laid her head back on the couch, tossing a blanket over herself and letting her thoughts drift into the flames, listening.

*

Tsura and Stefan talked a long time about all that had taken place before climbing in bed under a pile of covers. They were thankful to be on the other side of death, or so it seemed at this moment. "It is hard to believe I have you in my arms again, Tha...Stefan...we are so fortunate."

"We are so fortunate, yes," said Stefan.

*

Wren and Shae drove home slowly, mesmerized by the moon's play of shadow and light on the fields and hillsides. Arriving home, Shae touched the stucco wall of their house with great affection. "Our baby," she said. "It may take care, but will probably not die before we will."

"I feel that way, too, about the trees and flowers we have planted. We will pass everything on to someone who is now a child. I think we do love these things like some people love their own children. But then, perhaps I do not know what having children is really like. I only know that my love flows out to these living things and to our home and to you, Shae."

Inside, they put on music, danced in a slow, close embrace, letting the feelings settle before sleep.

*

Ayotunde was unusually silent. Keara turned back the covers on the bed, lit a candle, undressed, waiting for him to reveal himself to her. Finally, he asked if she was ready to bring Bryn back into the world.

"What?" she said.

"Bryn said that he had to be born to another family fairly quickly before the Earth's energetic shift. We could be that family. We could bring him back into the lives of Yaro and Saffi.

"You've got to be kidding...no...you're not kidding are you?"

"Bryn may be looking for a way back this very minute."

"No, I don't think so. Surely, he has to have some processing time. Don't you think so?" said Keara. "I believe I might need some processing time as well. Perhaps you are just caught up in the emotions of this incredible day and will feel differently in the morning. Having a child is serious business. A lifelong commitment. Wow.... However, I am very honored that you would consider having a child with me, very honored. It is just that I truly must think this over."

"You are right, of course. Of course. We must think this over. Shall we just sleep for now?"

"Yes, let us just sleep for now."

The Room

At home in Bryn's room, Saffi and Yaro slept in the bed which had held their child, slept surrounded by all things Bryn held dear, slept in their memories, slept in their dreams both realized and gone, slept in the arms of the strong one, for each thought the other to be strong.

Chewa took the night watch this time. She sat by the window, invisible for now, knitting. She always liked to knit and think, to knit and imagine things coming together in a new and beautiful way, to knit with many different colored threads so that the outcome would be a surprise, to knit with many different feelings so that everything got included. She liked to knit lives back together in exceptional ways.

The Guide

Bryn sat with his Guiding One who had steered the boat of his journey into the Higher Realms. The Guiding One showed him a large screen, something like a computer, but somewhat more organic looking. It was similar to the blocks he had seen in the Temple with Nimi. As the Guide touched the screen, Bryn could see the spiritual bodies of people he had known and read their feelings regarding him.

He saw that his parents, Saffi and Yaro, were in his bed just where he had left them. The picture was somewhat blurred, a little fuzzy, but radiant with light. Colorful rays emanated from the two bodies, each ray filled with loving thoughts for their son's journey. The light was so strong that Bryn was not tempted to look around the room with any longing. He just received this gift they were sending him with gladness in his heart.

Then his Guide moved his hand across the screen changing it to the room of Keara and Ayotunde. From Ayotunde's heart, there was a piercing ray of green and fuschia light coming directly to Bryn. It was almost overpowering. The Guide said, "Just breathe it in for now. You will understand it better later." Keara's colors were a bit dimmer and seemed to hover closer to her physical body.

The Guide gradually led Bryn through the feelings and prayers each of his Earth friends were sending him including the Little People and the spirits of nature, the animals and plants and all of the things that cared for Bryn.

"I am so fond of all these people," said Bryn. "Will I get to see them all again? And the animals? And what about Jampa and all the monks? Will I see them soon?"

"Yes, Bryn. The Earth is in the process of shifting her energetic frequency, thereby allowing all of us to have a much easier view of each other, and also to communicate without quite as much interference. As you know, you have promised to return to life for one more short period before that occurs. You have some choices in this matter. I will describe them for you. But first, get some rest. It was a fierce storm we went through together.

Kunchen will be watching over you tonight to make sure that you are comfortable here and to keep your dream body grounded, so to speak, for the night while you get used to being here. We have some of your favorite things here, thanks to a Mr. Nickolas; I think you know him. You will see them in your room. I will take you there now and return for you in the morning. It was a fine journey across the sea, mate. I will be your skipper anytime.

Temple Visit

Transported by their feelings for Bryn and abiding by his wishes that they maintain the perspective that he is off on a spiritual journey to a wondrous land, Saffi and Yaro ascend from their bed to the Temple of Love in their spirit bodies. Holding hands in front of the large doorway, Saffi says, "Yaro, this is the temple that I visited years ago in my dream. We were always going to come here together and have finally arrived."

"Let us go inside, Saffi."

A Guardian appears at the door. "Greetings. I see that you are holding your son Bryn in your hearts. He has just arrived safely and is now resting. There are Guiding Ones waiting to speak with you."

They are led down a marble hallway, so polished and brilliant that it is as if there are no walls, just shining light, yet there seems to be an underlying structure. As the Guardian escorts them, they can only perceive a swishing sound from his cape-like robe and see a glimmer of gold from his shoes. Even when he faces them, his features are difficult to distinguish due to his radiance. He is very tall with a commanding presence and deep voice.

They entered a room which felt circular, High Beings sat in a semi-circle before them. They were asked to be seated on a soft-cushioned white couch, also curved. They were almost overwhelmed by the intensity of these beings, even though the atmosphere was quite cordial and friendly.

"Welcome, Saffi and Yaro. You have given the utmost care and attention to our son, Bryn. Yes, we consider him our son as well as yours. His time with you has brought about many changes in the people whom he has touched, all with your help and guidance. He would have stayed with you for much longer had he not promised to assist one more set of parents and the people in relationship to them.

"His love for all humanity is very deep and many in this time are trying to make the leap which is required to pass through the gateway opening at the end of 2012. This is a subtle but important shift. After that time, you will see Bryn in his total exaltation and understand all that you have been through completely.

"We have brought you here because you are part of the foundation upon which the materialization of the Temple of Love shall take place. It is your sensitivity to Bryn and his needs that has allowed this to take place. Your dedication to each other and to him as well as to your spiritual integrity has been, shall we say, as mortar to the stones of the Temple.

"Each stone must be etherically constructed from acts of compassion. It takes many such actions to build a true Temple of Love in the present Earth frequency. You were without flaw in this regard. Thus, we are inviting you at this time to make full use of this etheric Temple for your pleasure and healing.

"Kalden, who has been working with your group on Earth, will show you around." These words seemed to be spoken by all who were gathered, yet must have been thought transmissions of their combined mind.

"We are humbled by your words, High Ones, feeling ourselves to be so much less than how you describe us. We are ever aware of our shortcomings as we strive to do good. Yet, we must believe you are sincere in your compliments for it could not be otherwise. We thank you so much," said Yaro.

"Thank you so very much," said Saffi.

Kalden appeared and escorted them to the Healing Rooms which had many pools of water, each a slightly different hue. Angelic Beings were present to be of assistance. Saffi and Yaro were told to return anytime they needed revitalization of their physical bodies or a fresh outlook on their earthly lives.

Kalden then escorted them to one of the libraries, saying that this was the Historical Room. They were welcome to review any of Earth's history that they had questions about. There were other libraries with different purposes, but these were off limits for now.

Then, they were taken to an Adoration Room and told that they could come here anytime they wished to make love to each other in a divine manner. Saffi was particularly curious about this room because she had seen the Temple sculptures in her prior dream. "May I ask a question?" she said.

"Of course," replied Kalden.

"I came here once in my dreams and saw many sculptures of people engaged in sexual activities. Can you tell me about these?"

"Yes. It is our belief that humanity, in order to uplift itself, must be shown images of loving activity, all kinds, from the cuddling of a child in father or mother's arms to uniting sexually with a chosen partner. At the present time, your Earth culture is permeating the atmosphere with images of violence. It is also combining things that you once thought sacred with lowly acts so that you lose faith that there is any purity in the world. These are destructive activities.

"The Temple of Love must show, in art, in music, in all activities, that there is a loving way of being. Your parenting behavior with Bryn as well as your love for each other through all of your everyday activities has lived up to this standard. Now, you are working with several others who have brought their own talents and loving actions to combine with yours in the building of an actual physical Temple of Love. This is a great achievement.

"All of the art will be created by this group of people and the others who will soon be attracted to this project," said Kalden. Now, choose which room you would like to be in for this evening of time."

Saffi spoke, "The Healing Room would probably be most useful right now as the last few days have been so intense and emotional."

"Yes," said Yaro. "That is my choice as well."

Kalden then led them back to the Healing Room and told

the Angelic Beings of their situation. Angel Leaf came to assist them. He brought fresh robes and slippers, told them to remove their earthly clothing and step into one of the healing water pools. He suggested violet first which may then change to a harmonizing green pool. He said that the water would take care of everything. Then, he left them to their privacy.

The Pools

"I remove everything...clothing, thoughts, worries, confusion, exhaustion...and step into this violet pool. It is warm and takes me down below the surface where, to my surprise, I can still breathe easily. I relax totally, seeming to glide gently down to incredible depths, impossible depths for a small pool in a building, yet I keep going down.

"The water is so comfortable it feels like air and I begin to experience myself in a violet-tinted landscape, very faery-like. I feel extremely light, as if there is little gravity here. I can dance and float up from the ground like a faery myself. Soon, I am dancing with other translucent beings, some with wings, some tall, some very tiny, all happily dancing in a small clearing in the woods.

"I spin and twirl and laugh. They do the same. We all fall like children to the ground, still laughing, the world spinning above us. I see a million green leaves swirling and suddenly I am swept up by them and tossed like a paper airplane into a mint green pool. Splashing, I go down again into deep water. This time very watery shapes appear to be people bubbling words toward me. The words say, "Saffi, Saffi," as if they are making up a song with my name.

"I feel them stroke my head and run their fingers through my hair. I begin to feel like a mermaid and chuckle at the thought. One approaches me and hands me a necklace with a shell attached to it, a very pearly iridescent shell. As I open my mouth to thank her, bubbles come out and everyone giggles.

"Suddenly, I am home in bed." This is how Saffi described her dream to Yaro.

"Saffi, I was there too," Yaro replied. "We met with High Beings in the Temple of Love. They complimented us immensely and gave us a tour of the building. Then, in the Healing Room, I took off my clothes and dived into a violet pool of water. It was much deeper than I expected. It seemed that I was under the ocean, not in a building at all. There were all kinds of sea creatures, but I was not afraid. They stared at me, but seemed to know just what I needed. They pulled on me here and there, dragged me along with them for awhile, did a few somersaults, and then left me to float.

"It was as if I were in a lagoon then with the sun shining above me. I just floated. The water seemed turquoise blue then changed to a deeper green. I just floated in heavenly peace. Then I woke up here in bed with you."

"I think Bryn is in good hands, Saffi. I know we will continue to have our periods of grief, feeling his loss from our lives, but I sense that we shall find him with us again soon somehow...in some way."

"Oh, I am afraid to hope for that, Yaro, but I am comforted to know that he is safe and well. The sun is rising now. Let us get up and engage the day."

News

"Wren, why are you listening to the news today?," asked Shae.

"Every now and then, I just like to tune in to see if I am immune to being affected by it yet," replied Wren.

"And the results?"

"Um, not quite yet."

"Grandmother told us not to look for results yet. They will come in time. Instead, we must keep our minds focused on the Great Land or kind, loving thoughts or thankfulness ... something positive and uplifting. If we hear of something bad happening, we are to respond with full compassion, right?" said Shae.

"Right. Yes. Sometimes I think I am 'being informed' by the news when, in fact, I am being manipulated," Wren smiled. "It is still easy to trick myself into believing that I can listen to forty-seven bad news items and not have an emotional meltdown somewhere in the depths of my being. Yet, as Grandmother said, we are designed to <u>respond</u> to everything we hear. That is our nature. And we want to respond in a helpful way. But, when we hear more than we can possibly respond to as a single human being, we have to squelch our natural reaction. So we store up negativity. This affects our health as well as our mood," said Wren.

"Come here to me and lay some more high thoughts on my tired mind," he said to Shae.

"You come here to me," said Shae. "Momma's gonna give you ca-an-dy," she sang and teased him out of his funk. She put on some dancing music and started telling him all the things she likes about him, all the things that have always turned her on.

Now, the room came alive. The lampshade tilted. The clock chimed. The rug got kicked into the corner...but didn't mind. The couch prepared itself to be moved or fallen upon. An umbrella fell off the stand. The dancers laughed and decided being naked was not necessary for their current passions to be expressed. Magazines fell on the floor. In fact, the entire landscape of the living room changed, starting to seem like a hot jungle of exotic monkeys screeching and leaping from limb to limb. You get the picture.

Return

     Roan went immediately to Yaro and Saffi's yellow house at the edge of town. Flooded with memories and questions on his flight from India, Roan was suddenly swept into a silent grief as he entered their home. A wave of compassion enveloped his whole being and he held both Yaro and Saffi close to him for as long as he could.

     Saffi said, "You two go outside now and be together while I arrange some things for the fire circle tonight at Kate-Amee and Reuban's house." There were many people coming to hold some of the burden of Yaro and Saffi's loss, to put into the fire all the feelings that might interfere with their higher spiritual understandings of what had taken place, and to affirm the importance and meaning of Bryn's life in their own lives.

     Yaro and Roan, outside now in the cool air only had to look at each other for a few seconds before they began their run. Running, running, putting the whole body into the feel of life flowing through it. They outran their concerns, their doubts, their fears. They outran the mind and all its wonderings. They ran until their hearts were beating to a grand feeling of oneness with all that exists. Oneness with Bryn, with each other, with this change of seasons, this change of life.

     "We never left each other, Yaro. It only appears that way in our physical form. I have missed you. I have missed everyone here. But when I meditate, I feel that I am still present with you. This life has had its hardships, but I see now that many of my own were caused by my learning to distance myself from things I didn't like rather than take action toward what I did like. I suppose joining the monastery was also a distancing, but it took this much of a separation for me to see myself.

     "Now, Bryn is separated from you physically, and though I can't imagine how hard this must be for you, I am beginning to learn. I am seeing that we come into this life, in part, to experience the physical senses. Some people need strong jolts of basic emotions, intense physical activity - fight, flight, fling down the women, fill the belly, scream, save things that are screaming. It is a level of experiencing 'power over.' And there are others who have come to discover and share the subtle senses while guiding those basic inclinations. I feel that we do that with our running.

"We are not in a race. We are not competing. Yet, we are giving our all to the physical experience at the same time that we allow our minds to shift into a higher gear. The basic experience of bodily power is still there, but something else has been added. I would like to do that with this grief. It must be experienced as the intense emotion that it is, but it can also be lifted to a higher level as it is released.

"I say all this, Yaro, to give you permission to scream or swear or cry or whatever you need to do for your body's well-being and your emotional completion."

Yaro turned his head toward the ground, pondered these ideas a minute, then lifted his head to the sky and screamed, "Bryn! God! Saffi! I want us back together! Bryn! I am trying to deal with this properly...I just need to 'lose it' for a minute. Ayeeeeee!" the scream soared out from his being. Then tears.

Roan joined him in the scream and in the tears. Just yelling at the top of their lungs to the Universe. Letting the feelings rip through all the 'should not's.' Then, they both collapsed onto the field. Quiet. The cardinals flew by. Always looking out for each other.

Baby Talk

Keara and Ayotunde could not help continuing their discussion about asking the soul of Bryn to come to them as their child. Was this preposterous? Egotistical? Beyond the call of duty? Does the world need another human being on the planet? Could we actually be good parents? Would we be able to continue our creative lives along with the responsibilities of child rearing?

What would be the role of Saffi and Yaro in this child's life? Would everyone know it was Bryn? Would we even know for sure? Does that matter? And what if Bryn were handicapped again in some way, a life-threatening disease or a mental malfunction? Differently-abled, yes, but can we handle that? And, do we want to bring someone into a world in such distress?
Do we even know what is right at this time or are we just reacting to the grief of the moment?

So many questions to consider and discuss. Keara said, "I want you to know how seriously I am taking your desire. I feel the intensity of it, yet I also feel its potential impact on our lives. It seems that you are shielded from that at this moment. I suggest we give this idea a week or two before we make our final decision, if, indeed, 'final' is the proper word. It is just that if we do have a child, I want him or her to come into a peaceful world, the Golden Age that we imagine is ahead, not the age of struggle and strife we have been wading through all of our lives."

"I understand, My Lady, I understand. I am just bathed in the feeling of joy that could come to us all if we thought Bryn could return to us in a new body, unencumbered by his previous ailment. He was a holy child. He was a holy child," said Ayotunde.

They kissed to seal their pact of patience on deciding this matter. If 'deciding' is, indeed, the right word. Then, they began their preparations for the evening fire circle, gathering instruments and ceremonial supplies, feeling peaceful now focusing simply on the present moment.

The Fire

    Seasoned old wood and sticks in a circle of stones.
    Take us down to the bones.
    We come with our voices of sorrow,
    of choices we made to involve ourselves
    in the lives of our friends whose strengths we borrow
    in our times of need.
    Let us heed the lessons learned,
    the blessings earned,
    Let us listen and sing
    and always bring
    our attention to the truth alive in the soul.

    Tonight, it is freedom
    to go past the event of Bryn's ascension.
    Freedom to recall the moment of reality
    we shared with him and mention
    the quality
    he brought to our attention.

    It may have been the day we caught the first fish
    or the sharing of our favorite dish,
    perhaps, the making of a wish as we gazed at stars above.
    What was that moment when we both knew love?
    Fire, free us from our hesitation
    to offer the fullness of ourselves to this occasion
    and to every time that we shall meet
    hereafter.

    Amen.

    This prayer was composed and read by Hartford Leith as the fire was lit. All contributed in their own way another gift of words or songs. Each gift dispelled their sorrow and concentrated their appreciation for life still left to be lived.

Nature's View

"I am so glad that the human beings are coming into our knowing," EC said as she wiped a tear from her eye. "They had so many lessons to learn. I did not think they would make it." Cascade was standing nearby watching the fire ceremony.

"I took Reuban out to the big field last night and spoke to him, in my way, of the greater body we all share. So many humans think that the sounds we animals make are our voices. But we communicate in much more subtle ways which are translated into words the human can understand by the mind of All-That-Is. Reuban knows this and trusts his time with me. I need make no noise whatsoever for him to know what I am thinking."

"Well," EC replied, "Reuban is one who spends a lot of time outdoors caring for nature. He has learned to pay attention to what is going on with us all. I wish that more humans would shed their fears of dirt and kneel down in humble service to this Mother."

Cascade nodded.

The night knew the power of fire to transform. It had witnessed gigantic fire clearings of entire forests, whole forests giving themselves release from the pollutions of humankind. Whole forests protesting the mistreatment of their kind. The night also knew also the ash left by fiery volcanoes became new soil, the land from which Morning Glories spring and life emerges once again.

Night watched over this small fire, listened carefully to its intent. Saw the shadow of the Phoenix hovering nearby. Night accepted the gifts the people brought to honor Bryn, carried them to the Sun to give back to the Earth the next day. Rounds of duty easily shared by all.

Women's Group

The day was brisk and sunny, one of those golden-tinted still green mornings of late fall in Indiana. The women of Grandmother's Circle arrived with their favorite foods to share, full of stories and laughter. So much happens in each life that it is nearly impossible to share the depths of one's responses and challenges while keeping all the fires burning - self's needs, family obligations, homestead maintenance, car repairs, gardening, cooking, cleaning, reading, writing, composing, crafting, celebrating, all the gestures of love that make life delightful.

Today, Grandmother says, "It is nearly the end of this transformative year. I think of it as an edge, like the edge of a page which must be turned. The story has been adventurous thus far; what will the next chapter bring? Usually, it is not an entirely new story, but a deepening or a completion of what has come before. This wondering about what comes next keeps us looking forward with anticipation of new possibilities.

"I would like us to refresh our minds on what we have done thus far, a quick summary, then focus on what is in need of completion before we can turn the page to the chapter we most want to be living."

Holding the Talking Stick, Keara began, "I see my life now as being very much about sexuality, all the different ways it can be expressed. I have listened to so many women who met extreme challenges in their sexual relationships, and I, myself, have had a wide variety of adventures, mostly good, thankfully.

"At this point, Ayotunde, my wildly enthusiastic partner, wishes that we could bring a child into the world, a very specific child, Saffi and Yaro's son Bryn who has ascended from this world only days ago. I don't even know if this is possible, but Ayotunde is so sincere about this that I must think it over carefully." No one responds verbally while the Talking Stick is being passed or held by someone else. This allows everyone a chance to simply be heard before ideas are shared by the group.

"I would say that my life has been a spiritual dance," said Shae. Movement, meditation and trying to form an ever-deepening relationship to the Great Being has been a constant theme. I feel completely at one with All-That-Is when I am beading, painting or dancing. However, I still feel some barriers between myself and other people. I want to sweep them into the bliss I feel inside myself, to give them tools to go into the ecstasy on their own, but also to share it with me.

"At the same time, I tend to criticize myself for this feeling of separation that sometimes occurs, thinking that if I were 'really holy,' the barriers would all dissolve by themselves. I suppose my goal is simply to become whole ... really holy."

Nola took the Talking Stick and said, "I feel a bit 'behind the times' in terms of my spiritual growth, partly because I am a few years younger than all of you, but also because I have been fully engaged in making a living and a home for myself and three sons until I met Hartford. Then, I acquired so many other interests that, even though the economic aspects of life are taken care of, now I am in school, have become a baker and am involved as much as I can be in all of your lives. So, I still feel too busy.

"However, this new 'busy-ness' is all very pleasurable, and I do not want to eliminate anything that I am currently doing from my life. Hartford has been a great teacher, supporter, and lover to me which is my greatest blessing. My painting is on the back burner, but I am creative in so many other ways, that I don't think this is a problem. My current challenge is to accept this fullness of life and just relax into it."

Kate-Amee took the Talking Stick next. "I have been so fortunate to be able to stay home with my children and Reuban all these years. We lucked out in getting an old farmhouse on a piece of decent land that did not cost us our lives. I spend a lot of time singing with the children and as they become older and more skilled with their instruments and voices, it beats performing on stage any day. I can be with my 'band' all day if I want to be. That is great.

"Currently, my thoughts head toward, 'What will the world

be like for them after they leave home.? How can we help them to live their own dreams? How can we continue to keep them from encountering 'the poisons' as we call them, spare them the errors that have plagued humankind during our lifetimes? Will these be magically gone at the end of this year?' I have my doubts, though I try to routinely shift my focus back to strengthening what we have going for us in the present and know the future will take care of itself."

Saffi solemnly took the Talking Stick as her mind was drifting into her seemingly 'lost' family now that her son, Bryn, was gone from Earthly presence. Everyone felt her dilemma and silently sent her strength.

"It is hard for me to imagine Bryn being in a different body in someone else's family rather than my own. Yet, that feels very selfish of me. Of course Keara and Ayotunde should welcome his spirit into their lives in whatever form it takes. And who knows what good might come from this arrangement for all of us. I think it is just too soon for me to think about this possibility. You understand?" There were nods of affirmation all around.

"My challenge right now is in deciding what is next for my life. What is my work now that I am not a 'mom.' I think that is all I can say at this moment."

The stick returned to Grandmother Tsura. "It has been my work to gather people together in common purpose, that purpose being spiritual, but also manifesting as something real on the planet. I have held different visions of what this material manifestation might be at different periods of my life. Now, it is being called a Temple of Love.

"Through all of the permutations of my plans and dreams, I think these words probably describe the overall theme of all the versions of what I have been doing. We have all participated together in making, as the monks have told us, the etheric stones of this temple. I am very proud to be part of this pile of building materials," Tsura laughs.

"Now that Stefan is with me, I know that he will be

sculpting art for the Temple. I expect that all of your artistic talents will be involved in many different ways as the project goes forward. Mine will be as well. The important thing, however, is this coming together of our creative talents, not whether or not a physical temple is ever built, though I hope that it is.

"Just as the template for 'the Healing Center' was given to us to inspire us to learn many healing techniques, to break down the limited thoughtforms our society was holding around health and disease, and to open us to higher frequency methods of creating our reality, so the Temple of Love also may be such a template. But, let us not underestimate its power.

"As a young woman, when the peace symbol was first placed into my consciousness, it gave me the strength to dramatically shift the course of my life. 'World Peace' was itself a template which gave an entire generation of people the idea that we could live in a world without war. Though still not everyone has adopted that point of view, you probably take the idea for granted. Yet, it was not always part of mass reality.

"World Peace. Healing. Love. This is where we are right now. It is not that people never loved before or never healed. It is just that it was not rooted in world consciousness. Now, it has taken root. It has helped many to overcome their prejudices of race, creed, color and sexual orientation. At this point in time, the polarities between the peace/healing/love consciousness and the fight-to-the-death fears still residing in others are very obvious and dramatic. It is the final round of polarity before smooth sailing.

"Many human beings have predicted this shift and have been working diligently to make it happen 'on time' in our time. We are some of them. Your life stories affirm this. Today, we are just reminding ourselves that the story is not over yet. 'Smooth sailing' does not mean we do not have to steer the boat. There are still waves and storms and new islands of experience that we will come upon. But we are strong. We are a skilled team. We will survive. Our lives have proven this as well.

We will make a world in which Nimi, Mirela, Nickolas,

Carlos, Aron, Dayo and all the children born into this world will be well. Our foundation is strong. God's work is already done. The Temple of Love has already shaped our lives and given us the children who have what it takes to build the next level of its construction. We have even been given children who are enlightened enough to take the ills of the world into their bodies, and, through what we perceive as suffering while enduring their handicap or illness, are able to calmly proceed with their lives until death takes them out of creation.

"We suffer our empathy for them and also are shored up by their strength and equanimity. Our suffering partly arises from the knowledge that our species, the human beings, seems to have created the conditions that caused their handicap. Our suffering is our deep regret in having done so as we see our human errors hurting someone we love. These young ones are great teachers and allow us to purify our heart chalices by loving them and inspire our conviction to change the world by cleaning up our mess and instituting more balanced ways of living. You have all given your lives to this process. Let us continue."

The talk continued long into the night, moving through its humor and tears, into feasting and rest. The season held its breath long enough to take in the women's offerings to the Four Directions, to the river Shemaya, to the sycamores and poplars and pines, to the creatures below and above, to the winds and fires and waters and earth. All the colors sparkled with dew until the sun licked them clean and covered them with night. All the creatures sung their songs at just the right times to soothe the soul of the world for one more day. All pray by their attention to life. And it continues.

Men's Meeting

It was not often that the men in the Circle met separately from the women unless there was a work project needing to be done. But all had been moved by Bryn's death and decided it would be good to process their feelings together, the man's perspective.

Hartford spoke first. "I am the eldest here, meaning only that I have more experience in terms of years in this life. I also have lost one loved person, my former wife, Evelyn. Since coming to the first meeting of Grandmother's Circle, meeting all of you, and meeting Nola, I see how I have been given another chance to create something wonderful.

"I have a second family, a devoted lover, more music to come through me, an architectural challenge to meet, and the kind of community I have never experienced before. It is a new and more spiritual focus. I count my blessings every minute that I am alive, knowing that statistically, I am likely to be the next to leave this Earth. I want to thank you all for being part of this wondrous opportunity to share in your lives. You are my symphony."

"Thank you, Hartford," said Reuban. "You are a fine example to me of a steadfast person, keeping to your creative and family pursuits, never wavering, as far as I can tell, from what you wanted to do in your life. I gain strength from watching you. You have raised two sons, now three more in process. I want to give you permission to pass on any of your child-raising wisdom to me as I raise my three children.

"Concerns for them loom largest for me right now. I am working toward the Golden Age, but I am not sure when it will arrive. 2012 is simply a date many of us have focused on to give our dreams a deadline ... a lifeline perhaps, if only to say, 'We are tired and we would like to accomplish this now.' Losing Bryn is a loss to all of us. He was a good leader for our younger ones. Yaro, what can we do for you?"

Yaro replies. "Fortunately for Saffi and I, Bryn consistently left us instructions that seemed to come from his High

Self. He does not want us to remain in sadness at his passing. I know he will continue to be with us in some way. I think the best any of you can do for us is to remind us of this. Just say, 'What does Bryn need from you now?' That will help.

And you can bring us some of the laughter that Bryn always brought to us. Otherwise, just be patient as we go through this grieving and re-orienting process. Again, I thank you all for standing by me in this time. I think we have certainly filled the etheric form of another stone for the Temple of Love. May we continue to build."

"You are magnificent, all of you," said Ayotunde. "You are the instruments through which the song of God is heard. After Bryn's death ceremony, I was overcome with the desire to father him back into this life so that Saffi and Yaro's joy would return. I am still willing to do so if the Spirit wishes it to be. I am saying this just to let you know the strength of Love to overcome all of my fears about having a child," Ayotunde smiles.

"I would have to alter my career plans, my travels, my life as the star of the show. My ego normally will not allow this, but Bryn...Bryn's spirit is so strong, all of this was overcome and I asked Keara if she wanted to bring Bryn back as our child. I think she about fell out of bed on that one," he laughed.

"Now, we are speaking about it more seriously, outside of my emotional response. I believe a soul can return quickly, especially into good circumstances or when there is a great need. Conceiving Bryn would be a privilege and a compelling ceremonial event. Keara reminds me, of course, that child-bearing is one event, and child raising is eight million more events. Yes, I must consider that. Can Ayotunde keep the wonder of it going throughout all the years of the child's life? That is the question I am pondering at this time."

Wren responds, "Ayotunde, you are quite an amazing person. Your talents go way beyond your musical abilities. You have such a fresh view of just about everything. I admire your intensity and love of life. I think you could make a great father, but it would definitely take a lot of your time. It might feel like a sacrifice. I would hate for you to lose your vibrancy, to feel confined. Also, I am not sure we need to bring Bryn back. We have many other children to teach and to love. They are all worthy of our attention. Perhaps Bryn is just giving us room to attend to them all more fully."

"Excellent points, My Friend, excellent," said Ayotunde.

Roan spoke, "I know I am living far away from here now, but I still feel myself to be part of this group. I think that we will all be guided day by day into our life's proper course, just as we always have been. Right now, I think that after Andret and Stefan speak we should offer Yaro our touch. Have him lie down, relax, and just channel our love into his energy field while we are all here together."

"As I am the newest member of this group," said Stefan, "I do not have so much to say about Bryn's life, but I know that his death has been a strengthening of our community. That is all I want to see now. I am here to help with the building of the Temple of Love. As a sculptor, you are all my models. You don't have to pose; you just have to be yourselves. I am sculpting loving actions, and I see before me seven men who are 24 hour-a-day loving actions. All I have to do is observe. Thank you for letting me do so."

"I am humbled. I am Andret, the humbled. You are my mentors. My fathers. I will do anything for you. Thank you."

They made a pad of blankets on the floor for Yaro. Andret adjusted the lights, brought in a pitcher of water from the kitchen and suggested they pass the pitcher around. "Each one hold the pitcher and send your prayer for Yaro into it. Then we will fill our glasses of shared prayers which will be carried by the water through our bodies making us all as one."

The water was passed. The cups were lifted. The water carried the love to all the bodies. Yaro rested on the blankets, closed his eyes to receive. The men chanted 'Om' for several rounds, then began to touch Yaro with the divine energy flowing through them.

    The woodstove fire crackled with warmth. The day extended itself so that there was plenty of time for such a welcome activity. The clocks were all willing to slow down. Phones refused to ring. The floor softened. Muscles relaxed even more. And even more. Words floated out now and then from deep, male voices, floated like birds landing on fences, vigilant birds, presiding over the fields of life like kings who know themselves and their places.

    Yaro drifted from the living room into the hall of kings, into the healing pools, into the sanctuary. God's arms. God's voices. God's way of things.

How It Happened

"Lead us into your heart tent, Saffi," said Grandmother, "so that we can be with you in your experience."

"I am alone, or so I think," said Saffi. "No one seems to have the same kind of thoughts that I have. The people around me talk of things I can see like food and weather, cars and clothing, children and household items. None of this seems important to me. I am wondering about angels and God and saints and how everything works, nothing that anyone else speaks of except in church.

"Yet, the priests and nuns speak as if everything magical happened long ago, never to be again. I want to go back or to find those holy people somewhere in my present life. It takes years and years, but finally I meet someone who is very different. I overhear a conversation between this person and a co-worker. His voice is exceptionally peaceful. I never see this person again, but his voice remains in my consciousness. It is something I subconsciously begin to track.

"I do not track the person, just the frequency his voice carried. I begin to meet others who match this voice quality. They are living a different life than I am living. Again, I don't know if I can fit in. But, I begin to make acquaintances. I observe, listen, discover that these people very sincerely care about deeper things, many of the things I have thought about since childhood.

"At a potluck gathering one day out at a communal farmhouse, I see how easily they share many things that usually are not shared in the mainstream culture. Cooking, child-raising, chores, even sexuality. They are unafraid of their bodies, unembarrassed. They enjoy touching, dancing, playing together, both music and games. I want to be like them.

"A butterfly lands on my hand and does not fly away. It stays with me for perhaps an hour even while I am driving home. The butterfly imparts its message that I, too, can change from what I have been to become what I wish to be. It flies away at the river

Shemaya, the crossing.

"It is not too long after that that I meet Yaro. He has the voice quality I have been following. He invites me to that place where the butterfly left me, just to sit, just to be. He is very much like the butterfly in that he is giving me so many messages in silence. He simply guides my attention to the important things, the deep things that are taking place. In nature. In ourselves.

"My wings begin to unfurl in his presence. I know now that in many ways I was doing the same for him though I did not know it at the time. In our intimate conversations, we shared our philosophies of life, often lying in a field looking at the stars and laughing. He always looked at me as if he cared about the invisible person, the one inside, the one that no one else seemed to notice.

"When I thought that he was moving to another state, I was very saddened. But, he changed his mind midway in his move and came back with more fervor than ever. From then on we have been inseparable. We did not want to have a child until we thought we knew each other's fullness of soul. That is to say, we wanted to feel certain that we each had everything it would take to raise a child with full love, devotion and skill. We wanted our relationship to be on solid ground before adding the surprise elements a child can bring.

"We wanted to be able to delight in those surprises, to meet them creatively and to be able to trust that our own relationship would float through this realm of new experiences. We also hoped that the world situation would improve. We spent years dedicated to this purpose before conceiving Bryn. Becoming part of this Circle gave us the kind of community we had been striving to create.

"Bryn came to us. We were able to celebrate life with him for twelve years. Now, like the butterfly, he has taken wing. I know that he has left us embedded with many messages we have not yet realized. These realizations will come.

"Now, I sit in my heart tent, surrounded by my circle of women friends. Each one is beautiful, talented, caring. Once again, I know that we are Goddesses, women of divine heritage. We are dancers stripping off our veils one at a time, revealing our divinity little by little to those who have eyes to see. We have partnered with men or women who do see. Their seeing allows us to remove one more veil.

"The more we recognize each other's godness, the more veils can be removed. Our dance will become even more powerful. Already, we take the hand of Nature. We kneel, bow down, turn gracefully, dive in, flow, emerge, climb, swing and kick up our heels with Her. And we are just beginning.

"We continue to grab the hands of other sisters, to stretch ourselves across continents, to arrange whole days of worldwide prayer together, to strengthen the web of our intentions. We are covering the world with ourselves. We are mothering the world. We are making love with life. Nothing can stop us now."

Shae's Dance

"I am twirling, spinning like the Earth itself. My eyes are closed as I look into my heart. My heart, with this attention, opens its doors and my spirit soars. In the sky, I unite with my sisters who are flying in formation. Our wings flap delicately. We drop feathers on the Earth, each feather brushing away a tear, sweeping away a problem that once was.

"I dive down and pick up lost children in my beak and take them to paradise. I take my huge white wing and scoop up pollutions, clearing air and water. I soar into the heaven-light where again I am cleansed, so that my journey can continue as long as need be.

"I spin down to Earth and become again a human being, dancing in the streets and houses, singing in the malls and traffic crossings, laughing in the churches and offices, stripping away false faces, worry and fear. I instigate spontaneous acts of kindness, giveaways, and fix-it-ups.

"I ride my motorcycle powered by cream puffs and let my hair blow in the wind. I hear music everywhere, all kinds, from all people. There is no one left who cannot play. The prison yards have been made into parks because weapons stopped working worldwide and people lost the desire to fight. I am welcome everywhere I land.

"I am fed. Every door is opened by one of you, my Goddess women, and I am truly fed.

Keara's Gift

"I take the fragrant nectar of my hoya flower to my secret laboratory where magically I reproduce its scent. Gallons and gallons of erotic, exotic flower power. I fill my pink Good Humus truck with jugs of the stuff and drive all over town spraying whole neighborhoods. Everyone drops what they are doing, falls in love with whatever they are looking at.

"I toss out pamphlets printed on tree-free paper saying, 'Permission Given' and I don't say for what. 'Use Your Imagination' it says on the back. And I drive on. I find Ayotunde and say to him, 'Play!' We visit each house with a song. We leave instruments on the front porch. We stand in the street and start the beat. 'Play!' we say. And they do."

Kate-Amee taps Nola and all begin to nod, yes, let's dance and sing and celebrate. In the spirit of the vision that is building, they rise up from the floor. Sounding. Swaying. Speaking whatever comes. Improvising a dance which overcomes the sorrow shared, builds on the wishes and dreams. "We do not have to do anything the same old way. We are the change. We are the power. We are the Goddess. All acts of love and pleasure are our ritual. We are the Mother of the New World."

And thus, the day was full of renewal, the rites of the Living Goddess. And the women talked and slept and saw each other as they are.

Emanations

All through the forest there came a feeling of elation as the radiance of the women and the men passed through the walls of their houses and drifted out over the land. The auras of the Little People were tickled just a bit as they felt the shift and they wondered if it might be time for celebration.

"I feel an unusual air," said EC as she woke the next morning. "I had better check on the Hill to see if something wonderful has happened." She put on her walking clothes, comfortable boots and a hat, picked up her willow basket and was out the door before George was out from under the covers.

It was a brisk day, fair and clear. EC pondered the history of the land as she walked, remembering how her own mother would point out the quality of light coming through the trees on the Hill in the morning and tell her that she had to learn the ways of all the creatures who lived along the forest path so that she could recognize their needs and make sure, as she grew older and took over her mother's work, that each living being had exactly what they needed that day.

She was not allowed to go fast or overlook anything. She was shown that every hollow and stump and gathering of leaves was a home for someone, each having its own integrity that must not be disturbed without permission. There were tiny beings like ants and beetles and large beings like very tall trees and rivers and all sorts of beings in between.

Each had a place it called home, and most had a time they preferred to be awake and a time for hunting, bathing, cleaning up and eating as well as making love. "Not everyone looks like you or me, EC," she was told. "The light of the Great Being spins out an infinite variety of forms and all must be respected. Our job is to keep things working smoothly in this forest.

"A place is a territory of meanings. Each species will find a different portion of the land to call its home and in which it will partake of its sacred activities. We Little People, close to the Earth as we are, have a mission to make sure that each group of beings has the time and space it needs so that all can live a full life according to their species' propensities. A view of the river, for instance is very important to the Pussy Willows. Squirrels like lots of branches of all kinds. Snake prefers piles of leaves and sticks for a home place, but loves to sun herself on a nice, flat rock. Humans take up more room and enjoy a warm sun and a tree to lean against. "You will learn the many, many other proclivities of all the beings that pass through our part of the woods as you grow up and accompany me on my route each day."

"Yes," thought EC, "I have learned these things. Since the disruption on the Hill when a good bit of the trees were removed by some humans with loud and dangerous equipment, I have had to help so many beings relocate. But now there is a small group of people committing to repair the damage and to work with nature to create a temple and its gardens with the intention of restoring harmony there.

"It can never be the same, of course, but if the changes bring about a new level of communication between the human beings who visit the temple and the forest creatures who return to the land, that will be a good thing. There were always humans who loved the Hill, who came for picnics or to watch the birds or view the river or sit in the stillness. They had respected the place for centuries. I don't know how it fell into bad hands.

"Since the funeral of the little light boy named Bryn, I have felt a deepening. Something big is taking place. I don't know what exactly, but I feel a goodness approaching." EC complimented the autumn honeysuckle as she walked by, waved to the red fox on the ridge, slowed down for a turtle crossing the road, and picked up a small geode to give it a little shine.

She heard human voices at the top of the Hill and paused to see if they were familiar. Yes, it was the monks. They seemed to be brushing the ground.

A Light Touch

With large peacock feathers the four monks were very lightly sweeping the ground.

"Good morning," said EC, "Might I ask what you are doing?"

"Good morning," they all replied. "We are assessing the state of life here, looking carefully to see what still survives and will make it through the winter. As we sweep with our feathers, we are also soothing the soul of the plants, bringing thoughts of comfort and sharing the ideas of how the Temple of Love might be built here. We need to give them time to decide whether they would like to be part of the temple structure or part of the garden or whether they prefer to end their life here at this time," said Chewa.

"Bryn has given his body to the Earth now and we have spread his elements in a sacred pattern below all the land. In this way, a bit of his grace goes to all the creatures here. Now, we are spreading the intention of Grandmother's Circle and offering ourselves as spiritual helpers in the plan. By early spring, we will know the answer from all the dwellers here," said Kalden.

"With a temple such as we intend, it is very important that there be agreement among all the species, especially when land has been disturbed such as this has. We must move forward in tiny steps, judging the impact of each step on the whole. The feeling generated must always be one of increased spirit in the place. Everything we do must contribute life to the space."

"How are you feeling here, EC?" said Kunchen.

"Oh, I felt a tickle this morning, perhaps it was from your feathers, I don't know. I am sensing that there is something very big taking place, something that will reach much farther than this forest boundary. I very seldom think beyond this forest, but I have heard that there are many, many kinds of forests and even larger rivers and higher hills. The birds are always bringing back stories that expand my thoughts on how things can be.

"My sense is that somehow we are being united with these

other places, as if a spider is weaving a web that will connect us in some new way. Could this be true?" said EC.

"Very definitely so," said Jampa. "There are numerous spiritual connections being made at this time. Every small segment of life is being uplifted to a new frequency. Even your work of picking up discarded items that humans have left on the forest floor is part of this process. You take a piece of so-called trash, cut out the letters, make new messages with an attempt to say something meaningful, and that is exactly what we are talking about. You have upgraded the trash to a meaningful object. Do you see?" said Jampa.

"It no longer has its former energy, shall we call it 'purchase me' energy. It has been uplifted to a message that comes from your heart. It is a very small thing, but every small thing contributes to the whole. And every small thing must be attended to before the larger transformation is made whole," said Jampa.

"I am beginning to see now," said EC. "I think I shall go home now and tell of this with my letters. Thank you for helping me understand that I am playing a part in this undertaking."

EC walked back home feeling connected once again to the Hill that she thought was lost and to all the human beings, spirit people and nature creatures now working on its restoration. She would have to ask the fliers if they saw this kind of cooperation happening other places in the world.

Juanita's Morning

As EC came to the old poplar home of Juanita, the woodworker, Juanita was busily carving.

"So early, Juanita, for you to be working already," said EC.

"The first pink ray of light summoned me this morning, EC. I found myself full of ideas and enthusiasm to begin something new. I thought I might try carving a statue of the boy who just offered himself back to Mother Earth. It may be somewhat abstract; I just want to capture the feeling of this event. You know, it has been so very many years since humans gave their bodies back to Earth, preferring to embalm them with toxic chemicals, put them in fancy boxes and then in concrete," said Juanita.

"Some bodies were burned. This meant the release of toxic fluids into the sewers and eventually the waterways plus the mercury, dioxins and other chemicals cremation releases into the atmosphere. Imagine the gas it takes to burn an entire body. Think of all the hardwood used in caskets, not to mention the steel and copper and concrete, all things unnecessary if the deceased is allowed to naturally decompose in the ground.

"I just want to make something to honor this new awareness the humans are having in regard to giving back to Mother Earth. Dust to dust, the Creator told us. The least we can do is let that be so," continued Juanita.

"I see what you mean," said EC. "I noticed that Grandmother had made a beautiful shroud for Bryn's wrapping. The men folk dug the grave by hand. I know the grasses will quickly seed themselves and birds will bring some flower seeds. Soon, it will look just like the rest of the forest, but will perhaps be a more fertile spot. Will you place your statue there?"

"Only if it will add to the spirit of the place. I shall have to see when I am done. If I am pleased with my work, I will take it there and glean the opinion of all the dwellers. I am sure I will then know the right action," said Juanita.

EC had never thought much about death. It was such a natural part of life that she had not known there could be a wrong way for it to happen. All of the forest animals immediately cleaned up any dead body, each species having their own idea of a 'good meal' and being happy to have found a feast. She wondered if the tiny bacteria that sometimes took up lodging in a live human body were not just hungry for their share of the dead? After all, it was only the very tiniest of creatures that were interested in eating human flesh. Could they just be angry that humans had stopped offering them their dead? She would have to ponder this at a later time as she was now at the leaf hut of Fred and Bonjockay.

"EC, how lovely to see you this morning. We want to invite you to a gathering of all the Faer ones in the clearing at twilight. I am making hickory nut pie and Bonjockay has gone to Reuban's and Kate-Amee's to borrow some fresh cream from their cow. We felt a stirring this morning and thought that the forest was hoping for a night of festive song and dancing," said Fred.

"I think we have all felt a change in the air. I will be glad to come, and I'll tell George. He has a few new tunes to play for you. See you there," said EC. "I will tell Carl too."

When she arrived at Carl's carefully woven house of reeds, he was not there. A note was on the door that said, "Speaking with fish. Back at orange light." EC smiled having taught Carl how to read and use letters like she did. She enjoyed the notes. They kept her from worrying or waiting. They were acts of kindness, just like Jampa said. She thought now that she might write a "Thank You" note to the monks for sharing their insights with her this morning. Yes, a thank you, something with large and friendly letters, curving and colorful. Yes.

Initiation

    Hartford came to the next meeting of the men with the request that they welcome Nola's oldest son, Carlos, into his manhood and into their group. "We have kept Carlos involved with the development of his art, constantly supplying him with canvas, paint, drawing paper, occasional professional workshops as well as music lessons... every way we could think of to channel his passions into creative work both to develop his interest and to steer him away from all of the usual temptations of the teenage years.
    "He is a very fine boy, but we see that he needs to be welcomed into his next level of involvement with the world. Hormones happen, as we all know. Life intensifies. He needs the direction of all of us, not just this 'old guy named Hartford.' In the group we have a range of ages and experiences, and speak with different voices of perspective. I would love for him to become part of our adult conversations and responsibilities."
    "Absolutely," replied Reuban. "I know that each of us would have benefited from a group of male elders at times in our lives. Let us come up with a significant ceremony for Carlos' initiation."

    The men brainstormed many ideas from tribal to avant garde. They finally decided on something they called "Balls and Staff." Wren volunteered to go into the woods and find a good stick to shape into a walking staff. Hartford would purchase a dozen or so soft rubber balls. "Here is how I see it," said Ayotunde.
    "We form a circle including Carlos. We each have a ball except Carlos. One by one we speak out a problem that an adult male faces in the world, letting the ball be a symbol of that problem. We ask Carlos if he is ready to catch that ball. If so, we toss it to him. If he catches it, fine, he has accepted his response-ability. If he does not catch it, we put it aside. We will give him another chance later, but we make note of the balls he misses.

"After everyone has tossed their balls to him, we can tell him that we see his power or talent in each of those situations. Perhaps the balls can have symbols on them signifying the issue he has 'caught' and the talent or skill required to deal with it. For the balls he did not catch, we can discuss ways to strengthen the quality needed for the issue and give him a chance to catch the ball again. After he has caught all of the balls, he can legitimately say, 'I have a lot of balls,'" Ayotunde laughed.

"I suggest we then take turns engaging in improvisational dancing/wrestling with him so that he feels our physical strength and we feel his. It must be real, not violent, not wimpy...real...so that we do show strength but also sensitivity.

"Then, when we feel satisfied that he sees us truly as men and we see him truly as a man just like us, we break, take a drink of water, return with his staff. We meditate, imbuing the staff with our own powers. Then we offer it to him as a gift in recognition of the wisdom and experience he now carries.

"Incredible, Ayotunde. That will be a very empowering ceremony," said Wren. All agreed. They continued to discuss the details of when, where, time of day or night and whether to keep the ceremony secret and magical. Each left the meeting thinking of their own life challenges in their teenage years and refining the way they would speak of these things to Carlos.

Stefan recalled situations of being overpowered by his older brother and made to do dangerous things. Yaro remembered the push into the society of high finance that was so totally against his gentle nature. Reuban flashed back to his longing to be in the theater but feeling no opportunities for such a career for a farm boy. Wren pondered how serious he was as a child, trying to do the right thing, yet not easily finding a direction that felt comfortable. Ayotunde recalled so many friends forming lifetime relationships with drugs, relationships which sapped their energies and enthusiasm for life. He wondered what it was that made him go after the enthusiasms instead of the substances.

Hartford thought that life was easier in his youthful days. One simply did the next thing that was expected by family, church and society. The world seemed very local back then. Not quite as many distractions. Not quite as many enticements to 'greener pastures.' Not quite as much sexual liberty. He had met Evelyn in high school; they got along fine. Like most of their friends, they married, found jobs, bought a house, had children, raised them. It seemed fairly straightforward.

In the early 1960's, houses were cheap, fuel was cheap, cars were cheap, the economy was in good shape. There were fewer opportunities to do something "outside the box," but there were also fewer expectations that one <u>should</u> do something outside the box. The boxes were comfortable for white, middle class males. A little less comfortable for white middle class females. Very much less comfortable for people of different colors or religions or sexual identities. But, for Hartford, life was pretty good.

Then Evelyn died. Perhaps, that could be the issue he talks about with Carlos. "Loss. Of course! Carlos has already lost his father. He must have gone through very similar feelings as I did. How have I not been sensitive to this before? Loss. Abandonment. Aloneness. Confusion. Of course."

Hartford could see that the easy solutions to situations of loss, especially when no one seems to understand your feelings, include alcohol, drugs, sleep, withdrawal, and in the end, soul death. "But Carlos is an artist. Carlos can paint his feelings, just as I expressed mine in music. I must talk to him more about the feelings he is trying to express in his art. How could I have not seen this so clearly before? I must just be thankful that I see it now."

Andret did not yet feel himself to be a man and was unsure of his strength or even how to define his challenges. He wanted to please, and usually could please others. Everyone liked him. But he did not have his own life yet. He loved these men. He loved all they had done. Yet, their accomplishments seemed to him way beyond his abilities. He was learning farming and a little bit about music and liked the activities that the others created. He was glad that he was welcome. But something was missing. He had had sex with women...girls really. No one like Keara or Shae or the others. Was there a right person he had not found yet? Perhaps he needed an initiation into manhood just like Carlos even though he had lived nearly twenty years longer.

    The monks were watching...listening.

Following

"Follow him," said Chewa. The four monks flanked Andret as he walked towards town. He was not heading home but to The Spot so that someone else would be leading the evening and he could just follow. Join the crowd. Listen to others play. Watch others dance. Respond...as usual.

"Capture his attention," said Kunchen.

Immediately, a commotion could be heard in the alley. Andret saw shadows of a struggle and heard a moan. He ran instinctively toward the trouble. There on the ground was a wounded young man only partly conscious. Andret's heart was beating fast, his mind seeking help. He had no car. He did not want to leave the fellow laying there alone. Surely, someone would come by soon if he just held the man.

He sat down, carefully lifting the shoulders of the man so that he could cradle him somewhat in his arms. "The guy is probably dying. What should I do. Love him. Who is he? Who cares. Love him. How do I love him? Meditate. Send him strength. Hey, fellow. Hey, I am here with you, whoever you are. I am here. I am loving you. Can you hear me?" Andret was crying now, crying for his own inadequacy.

No one came along. Andret let the tears flow, holding the man. "Don't die," he said. "Don't die. Help me." Then, he thought, "What the hell am I saying...'help me'? I am not the one who needs help, this guy is." Then, he cried some more.

The dark alley mellowed into a small street of old red brick buildings, light in the distance, stars overhead. Trash cans and boxes softened into cushions for Andret's back. The wounded man's body was warm, very muscular, peaceful, as if he were sleeping. Blood on his shirt was no longer frightening, but seemed like a sign of life. It matched the blood now on Andret's shirt. He touched it. "Blood brothers now, I guess," he said aloud.

"Yes," said the man in his arms. "No one has ever held me like this. No one has ever cried over me."

"Shhhh," said Andret. "I am here with you and I will stay as long as you need me."

The man had not yet opened his eyes, spoke with them still closed. Kept them closed. Did not want to see who this was holding him. Preferred to imagine it might be God or, at least, a stand-in for God. Was willing to die in God's arms, this person's arms, if dying was at hand.

"I don't have a car. I am thinking that someone will soon walk by and notice us, and we can get you to a hospital," said Andret.

"No, no hospital," said the man. "No, I can die here. It's alright. I have nothing to live for. I just want to live this last moment in these arms, the arms of kindness."

"I am here for you," said Andret as he adjusted his body to find a little more comfort on the ground. "Can I make you more comfortable? Can I help you in some other way?"

"Shhhhh," said the man.

They sat a very long time in silence. Andret felt the beating heart of the man. Wondered if he was seriously dying, how bad he might be injured if not, whether he could hold him as long as he might be needed. Right then, he decided, "I will do whatever it takes. I am love. That is all I need to be."

The four monks were not far away. They knew exactly what was taking place in both of these people. It was exquisite. They were in awe of the Great Being, the infinite wonder of life, the beauty of the smallest acts. They watched quietly, sending a little support to Andret's back muscles.

No one came by. Both men were lulled into trance by the unresolubility of the situation. Their consciousnesses left their bodies as their spirits journeyed far beyond the Earth. There, in the non-time, they met again.

"I am Arjana. I have died in your arms before."

"I am known now as Andret. I have been searching for you. I ask that you do not die this time."

"This time I will not die," the stranger said.

Then, they were back without conscious awareness of this brief interchange between their souls. Arjana opened his eyes. "You are God, my god, you have saved my life. I am going to be alright. Help me up."

"Wait, wait, go slowly. Are you okay? I have been holding you a long time, hoping someone would help us, but no one came. Can I help you to a doctor or something?"

"No, no. I am fine now, sore but fine. I was attacked. He stabbed me, but I brushed the knife aside, so it is not deep. I think it was the loss of blood that put me out. You saved me. Somehow, you stopped the bleeding. How can I repay you?"

"I have already been repaid by your appreciation. Can I walk you home or somewhere? Can you even walk?," said Andret.

"Help me up."

Andret put his arms fully around the man, Arjana. His body felt very familiar, so very familiar. Arjana hung his arm over Andret's shoulder, a small but strong shoulder.

"I will think 'light,'" Arjana laughed.

"Yes, be as light as you can be," laughed Andret. And they hobbled out of the alley onto the street.

"People will just think that we are drunk," said Arjana. "Put your jacket over my shirt so the blood will not be noticeable."

"Where are we going?" asked Andret.

"We are going home. I mean, I live just a few blocks from here, turn down this way."

They came to an old Victorian house in which Arjana had an apartment, two rooms and bath. It wasn't a bad place, just small and somewhat barren. Arjana fell to the couch, exhausted from the walk. "Don't leave just yet please," he said to Andret.

Andret replied, "No, I won't." He could not leave even though he thought maybe he should. He did not really know this person. Or did he? His curiosity held him. But, it was more than that. He actually loved this person. How could this be? How could love happen in just a few minutes? Even though he tried to channel cosmic love to this dying man in the alley, now it felt like real human love somehow. How could it shift so dramatically? Neither recalled their timeless journey while their bodies lay in the alley, but they did recognize the shift in feelings.

"There is some coffee in the kitchen," Arjana said. "You can make some for us if you like."

"Yes, I will," said Andret, glad to have some minor distraction from the magnetic pull to engage more deeply with Arjana. He clunked around the kitchen opening cabinets, searching for cups, coffee, a pot, turning on the water. The kitchen woke up from its senseless slumber. A new voice, a new presence. Who is this?

The stove noticed a difference in the touch on her knobs. The sink winked. The refrigerator cleared its throat and expelled a few ice cubes into its container. The toaster wondered about breakfast, would it be for two? The cups sent the message, "Choose me, I'm special." The silverware drawer decided not to stick this time. They all waited for the next move.

In the living room which was also the bedroom, Arjana had lost consciousness again. Just sleep. Andret came in with two cups of black coffee asking Arjana if he would like cream or sugar or anything added. Then, he saw the sleeping prince. He did look like a prince as Andret really looked at his face just now. A very fine-looking young prince. He did not look like a tough kid or a fighter. He wondered about his age, how all this happened tonight, the history, but nevermind. Here is the coffee.
He gently tapped Arjana's shoulder. "Want to have some coffee?"

"Oh, oh yes. Just help me to sit up please," for he had slumped over on the couch.

Andret held this beautiful prince once again until he was sitting up straight. Their eyes met for just a moment. An endless moment. Then, embarrassed, they took their coffee cups. Andret made a toast, "To life."

"To life," said Arjana. And they drank the hot, black drink

and felt it go all the way down.

"I have nothing else to offer you," said Arjana.

"That is not quite true," said Andret. "You have already given me quite an evening. I don't know what to make of it yet."

"Do you want to stay here tonight?" said Arjana. "You said back in the alley that you would stay as long as I needed you. I still need you. In fact, I may always need you."

Andret pondered these words. How to respond? "Arjana," he said. "I don't want you to get the wrong idea. I wanted to help you. You were hurt. I was trying to do the right thing. I don't want anything from you. I'm sorry if I gave you that impression."

"No, Andret. You did not give me that impression. I am just confessing to you that I have never experienced the feelings that I had tonight. There was an energy coming from you that I never felt before. Then, there was something in me. At first, I thought I must be dying, maybe I have gone to heaven and this is some angel holding me. Then, I realized, no, it is just another human being, but he does not seem to want anything.

"The person that stabbed me wanted my money. Actually, took it. I don't know why he stabbed me; maybe out of fear. Then, you came. You held me as if I were your lover or your brother or your son. I have not had this kind of family before. All at once I knew what I had been missing. I mean, the missing piece was given to me. I wanted to sleep in your arms forever. That is my confession. You gave me something I have needed all of my life."

"Arjana, something has happened here tonight. I am also changed. I feel as though I have always known you...and loved you. My mind wants to stop me, give me warnings about getting further involved. But, I am tired of listening to it. It has been in charge way too long. I want to love someone totally. That is my confession."

Arjana reached out for Andret and Andret, as though he was a drop of water coming over the great falls, pulled by the current into the deep pool below, flowed into Arjana's arms, the muscled arms of the prince of peace. All the feelings intensified.

The peace deepened until it reached the holding place of tears. They both cried and they both surrendered to the crying and surrendered to the comfort and surrendered to the longing that was in them. Their bodies finally recognized themselves. Every muscle and bone said, "I am real. I am a person. I am a full person. Someone loves me. Someone loves me just because I am."

"Let me bathe you," suggested Andret after they had briefly slept. You are bloody and I am too. Let me touch you in ways that counteract the violence you have experienced."

"Andret, yes, that is just right. We are empty now, are we not, of all that would block us from knowing each other. The gate is open. No one has ever entered my garden before."

"Nor mine," said Andret.

The bathroom became a holy place. A place for cleansing souls. The old tub filled with clean, hot water. Tile walls glistened. Towels puffed themselves up. Soap slid off the rack. Steam rose and kissed the ceiling which had not been kissed in a very, very long time. Wallpaper soaked it up, wished it could peel off its layers. Mirror was totally fogged. Sounds of splashing. Sounds never allowed to emerge before. Bodies freed of wounds. Bodies as slick and smooth as when they were first bathed by the cosmic Mother. Bodies lifted as they were made to be lifted by the cosmic Father.

"We can do so much for each other," said Arjana.

"I think we have begun," said Andret.

Coaxing Life from the Ground

"We must go again to Bryn's gravesite, Stefan," said Grandmother Tsura. I want to thank all of the nature beings for their acceptance of Bryn's body and their participation in our ceremony for him. Because we have designated the area for a special purpose, we have initiated it as a being in itself. It now has a life that is slightly different than the life it had before as simply a part of the park.

"We have given birth to it as a unique entity and must establish our relationship with it. I am contemplating naming the area 'Heart of the Beloved,' if everyone agrees. The name will help us all to treat the area, and thus anyone buried there, with deepest respect. It will remind us that this is a holding place for our love, our very own flesh and blood passing through it in the form of the body laid to rest, just as our blood passes through our physical heart.

"It will also help us see the entire temple site as being alive. It will feel whole with a center and boundaries, just the same as we feel whole when we honor our spiritual heart and recognize our boundaries as individuals yet know that we are intricately linked with all that surrounds us."

"Yes, Tsura, let us go to the temple site. I know that each thing we do there strengthens the whole. I see the same phenomenon when I sculpt. The more that I see every small part of the figure as a wholeness in itself and make it pleasing to my soul, the more it enhances the entire sculpture. Nothing can be left to happenstance. Even the spaces in between an arm and the body, for instance, must be pleasing.

"There is spirit latent everywhere, in empty space and in substance. Our job as artists is to bring that spirit into view, to bring it through into materiality so that others will also see and feel it," said Stefan.

"I find that spaces speak to me. I walk into them and they show me visually exactly what they need," said Tsura. "Sometimes I am not capable of achieving what is needed. For instance, by myself I cannot build the Temple of Love. I can only encourage compassionate actions which strengthen the field of life there. This is what the four monks have described as building the etheric forms of the temple stones.

"The vision will seem to hang in the air when I am present at the site, and it may hover there for years and years if it is something large. It may also hover there if it is a very small thing that no one has bothered to implement. A rock that is in the wrong spot will just keep feeling out of place to us until it is put where it belongs. Where it belongs is that place where it causes the whole area around it to feel just right to us.

"We tend to separate ourselves from these feelings, thinking that we are just making them up, that they are merely our personal preferences or ego-motivations, but, actually, we are receiving direct communication from the space itself. The wholeness is trying to emerge. The Great Being is trying to say, 'Here I Am,' let my luminous presence be activated," Tsura continued.

"So many people have learned not to trust their imaginations or to discount them. They do not realize that it is the most powerful gift we have been given. It connects us with all of the invisible realms. From these realms we create our material world. All inventions and ideas come from 'nothing.' Actually, that 'nothing' is the wholeness. The wholeness is constantly trying to fill our needs and the needs of all beings.

"What we name something - a person, a site, a star, an experience, anything - effects it greatly. We accept many names for our physical experiences of things. For instance, to some, a tree is a tree; to others, a tree is a sycamore or an oak or one of many other species. To some, a tree is so many board feet of lumber or a stack of cord wood. To still others, a tree is a complex structure of cells and life processes.

"It is the same with food. Some people speak of apples and potatoes and bread. Others talk about all food as carbohydrates and proteins and other chemical names. Still others think of food in terms of its calories or its effect on their bodies. We accept all these ways of describing ordinary material things, but when it comes to naming things of the invisible or spiritual dimension, people are frightened by the names we use.

"Talk of faeries or wizards or God or angels or nature spirits or guides or goddesses and many people are dismayed or defensive. Some even become violent. Yet, we cannot see a carbohydrate any better than we can see an angel. All we have done is give what we do see or feel a name. Then, that name guides our interactions forever after unless we make a conscious decision to change our minds. Changing our minds takes discipline, however, not something that is easy for all.

"I much prefer the magical names of things. It allows my life to feel very rich and full of welcome surprises. My reality is filled with the Great Mystery because I allow nothing to be the absolutely final word on anything. I leave the door open always for new possibilities that I might enjoy even more. When Tha died, he helped me to experience more profoundly that 'he' is everywhere. If I love anything or anyone at all, I will be loving him.

"As an individual human unit, just like one of your sculptures, he can never be duplicated exactly. I could not pretend that someone else would be exactly the same in every way. But, I could open myself to accepting the love, the life force, the energy, that comes my way every day from every single thing I encounter. The form of his human body was simply that, a magnificent piece of equipment so-to-speak, but a limited expression of his wholeness. That wholeness is now revisiting me in a new form, you Stefan," said Tsura.

"You have given me your name and some details that we call your life history, but these are simply stories that we tell ourselves in order to shape our present day experience. The only way one's full life history could be known would be for us to learn everything about everything that ever existed, from the beginning of Time, if indeed there was a beginning. If one takes this far enough, one's mind can only collapse into the God-field, into infinity, into the magic of the Great Mystery."

"Yes, Tsura, life is basically that which happens between our visible actions and the world we cannot see. When we strengthen that relationship instead of denying it or keeping it within the parameters we learned in Sunday school, we experience ourselves as one with all things. A deeply satisfying moment.

Coming Alive

The small clearing in the woods where Bryn's body had been laid to rest, was gradually awakening to itself. It had been sung to, gifted, swept with straw and feathers and the elements of an entire human body had been placed within it so that it could utilize them once again for the purpose of ongoing creation.

As the clearing began to feel this fresh life force of attention shaping its destiny, it began to draw other compassionate actions to itself. Grandmother and Stefan came with thankfulness asking if it would like to be named "The Heart of the Beloved." This so pleased the clearing that a shower of golden leaves fell from the surrounding trees upon them.

The clearing knew that it was not yet all that it would someday become, but it looked forward to the events that would cause it to mature into its full divine expression.

Not Far Away

In another clearing down in the valley, the Faer People were gathering as they often did on nights the moon was full. Sticks had been arranged for a fire to keep them warm. The hickory nut pie was placed on the table along with creamy squash soup, fresh bread and apple cider. After the lifting of the cups to praise the day and the feelings it had engendered, everyone helped themselves to the nourishments.

Then, the music began. Little People and Faer Folk alike all loved to play. Songs drifted out, carried by the wind to anyone quiet enough to listen. Some songs wandered up to the Hill and swooped down to kiss The Heart of the Beloved. Other tunes danced along the ground, rolling down hills and up again on the other side. Some joined the water in its flow and headed for faraway places.

Each song had a life of its own and could establish itself in a person's consciousness, eventually being shared with other people it had not met before. And, if it was very moving or funny or easy to sing and play, it might be shared with more and more people, eventually becoming a cherished folk tune and remembered for a long, long time.

As Nimi drifted off to sleep that night, she began to be carried by a tune. The melody lifted her into a dream in which she visited the Hill again, stopping first at the Heart of the Beloved, leaving a small gift she had made, then going to the edge of the Hill overlooking the river Shemaya where she and Bryn had first entered the Temple of Love together.

"Bryn," she called, as she walked alone down the bright marble hallway.

"Nimi," she heard. "Nimi, I am here. Come quickly and I will show you what I have done."

Bryn took her hand and led her to one of the temple stones which embodied an act of compassion. As he rubbed its surface, the scene inside came to life just as it had when they visited the Temple before. In this scene, there was a dark alley. Some violence was taking place.

"I had been instructed to observe the people of Earth who live in our town, Nimi, and to watch for any situations where I could be of help. The Guides told me that because I had acquired a competency in kindness and helpfulness, that I could impart this to another living being if it was needed.

"Look closely. A young man named Arjana was being attacked by another man with a knife. As soon as I saw this I gave Arjana my strength to brush him aside. He was still wounded, but his life was spared. Then, Andret came to his aid. At that moment, I was no longer needed because Andret had the qualities which were then called for in the situation.

"I was told that I had done well and not to be concerned that Arjana was still injured. The Guide said that the injury was needed in order to facilitate the meeting of Arjana and Andret that very night. The Guide also informed me that things are proceeding in the best possible way due to both the brushing aside of the knife to preserve Arjana's life and the injury which united the two men.

"This is the work that I am currently involved in. I wanted to let you know so that you are certain that I will be with you if you are in need of any help. I will offer you my kindness and proper response to the situation.

"I must go now, Nimi, back to my work. I will meet you here again soon. Know that I am always nearby. Sleep well my friend."

"Oh Bryn, thank you for coming to me in this way. I will write of my experiences and send them off to you by way of the four monks so that you are also aware of how my life is going. That way, I will not interrupt your work. I shall look forward to our next visit. Good night, dear Bryn."

The warm covers welcomed the dream traveler back to her bed, safe in her room, moonlight and faery tunes wafting through the windowpane. Mirela slept nearby with her rag doll held in her arms. Nickolas cuddled in his furry blanket with his toy red dog. Reuban lay near Kate-Amee feeling lulled into a very restful sleep by a hint of distant music floating in. Kate-Amee danced in her dreams, warmed by a fire in the woodland glade. The house kept its doors tight against the cold, but let the breath of sound sift in, just a small fresh wind coming through at window's edge. Just enough.

  All the people in the household felt the fullness and completeness of having just enough. Enough time to sleep, to dream, to walk in wild places, to feel the welcome of home, to care about everything happening there. Just enough was always plenty.

The Search

Wren decided to get up early, take a long hike, look for the branch from which to make the staff for Carlos' ritual. He liked the morning light, the quiet that hovered before people started going to work and all the activities of the day. He packed some trail mix, gloves, a pocket knife and his journal. Shae had often read to him from hers, and he liked the idea of chronicling life's experiences. The written word often came out more poetic than the spoken word; plus, people sat back and relaxed into listening to something from a book, unlike most conversations where, if you were lucky, you had the opportunity to say a couple of sentences before being interrupted.

In the kitchen, he quietly made himself a fried egg sandwich and left a note for Shae. "Be home by supper, hiking to look for Bryn's staff. Love, Wren." Not exactly poetry, but, hey, it's 6am.

There were plenty of woods. Where to go? The sun seemed to be rising most noticeably on the road to the glen. He drove through a pocket of fog, Earth taking her morning breath. He breathed out his prayer that he might be guided to just the right piece of wood for Carlos. He thought about manhood. Going from that period of boyhood freedom in which life was jump out of bed, grab some food, go outside and create an adventure. School days dampened that, but boys were good at working around, alongside and beyond the rules.

Someone else, usually parents, took care of all the basics: keeping a roof over your head, clothes on your back and food in the pantry. No bills. No worries...at least if you could swing the tests at school. When that bell rang, you were free again and ran straight ahead to the next adventure. Then, something started to change. Some of your friends got interested in girls in ways that you never thought of before.

As the days went by, of course, you became very interested

yourself. There was a lot of talk among your friends about doing it. The big IT. "But, I don't feel like that was really my introduction to manhood, just a map hinting at the territory ahead. Stalking that territory was the true 'becoming.'"

"Adults pushed me to direct my studies toward a goal, one that would eventually provide enough money to take care of my life needs. My body prodded me to find a partner, sexual and desirable in every way. My mind wanted to learn new things. My emotions went every which way. It was definitely like climbing a mountain. Peaks, valleys, interesting overlooks. A staff imbued with the wisdom of male elders would certainly have helped."

Wren pulled off onto the gravel side road, put on his pack, locked the van and headed into the woods. He imagined what life might have been like if, as a boy, he could have walked into some enchanted woods where magicians and wizards lived. A place in which the Ancient Wise One was waiting for him with a strong brew that would open his mind and set him on his proper course of life. Then, the Wise One, wizards and magicians would take their turns teaching him the skills needed to travel the dangerous roads of life.

He would have a sword, fine leather boots, maybe an intelligent and faithful dog or even a hawk or a twelve point buck as a companion. They would communicate psychically and share their powers at every turn. Enjoying his fantasy, Wren sat down under a maple tree and took out some trail mix from his pack. "Great Spirit of this woodland, I open myself to your guidance on finding a proper staff for Carlos and to all the other wonders of this day. Thank you." He offered a bit of the mix to the spirit, tossing it gracefully to the ground. Then, he closed his eyes just to tune in a little more.

The four monks were waiting and emerged from behind the trees. "Wren, your fantasy is your reality, for we have been with you a very long time. Perhaps, we should have dressed more flamboyantly," said Jampa. "Your challenges were necessary steps in your spiritual growth, and at each turning point, we led a human being into a role that would compliment your situation and encourage right action.

"Remember when your family had to move to a new city and, though you were put in a position to have to make new friends, you were also put in an atmosphere of political awakening. This led to your learning how to avoid going to war. As a conscientious objector, you were given community service with people who brought out your love for nature and instructed you in ways to correct environmental disturbances.

"You met Yaro and took a magical substance not unlike a wizard's brew that shifted and expanded your consciousness. Another friend, or shall we say Wise One, directed you to the class at Shae's house where the beauty of the dance lured you into even higher consciousness. You have not been without your elder's guidance even though you have not always recognized the map that was handed to you. At least, you traveled the territory."

"I'm sorry," said Wren. "Of course I have been guided. I am deeply grateful for all that I have at this time in my life. Now, I just want to be a Wise One for young Carlos, and others, should they come along."

"So it shall be, Wren. So it shall be," said the four monks and disappeared behind the trees.

Wren continued his walk and his inner talk. "Sometimes I am really an idiot. I didn't mean to insult my mentors, the four monks and all those who have helped me along my way. Okay. Done with that criticism. At least I am getting better at stopping this negative self-talk. Okay. Trees, here I am. Guide me."

Turtle wandered onto the path, stopped, glanced up at Wren, continued. Hawk called down a greeting. Squirrel scampered by, dropping a nut. Came back, retrieved it. Wren pulled out the Trail Mix again and left a few more nuts for his nature friends. He heard other scrambling in the woods but did not see the deer it might have been. He went in that direction.

The Branch

Juanita woke up early that same morning. "I feel a call," she thought. Instantly, she was out of bed and into the forest. It was always when she began walking that the words would come. "Man." "Manhood." "Walking Tall." "Strength to make the passing." "Unbreakable." "Unstoppable." "Polished." She went to her "saving place" and retrieved an exquisite maple branch with a slight twist at one end. She remembered setting it aside about a year ago to dry out. "Perfect," she thought.

"May I take you?" she asked. "I think that someone needs all of the qualities you possess. The branch felt ready. Not knowing if the seeker of the branch would know how to carve it properly, she decided to rest it near her home so she could assess the person's skill level and ability to pay attention. If he paused long enough, she could transmit important information to him. But, so many humans just take and run. Once back home she set the staff down outside and went in to put on some tea and wait for the sound of footsteps.

About half a cup later, she felt the approach, not of footsteps but of consciousness. This was a good sign. The closer Wren got to Juanita's dwelling, the better she felt about him. His intentions were good. This stick was for a very special occasion. He seemed to be one with a love for the natural world and a good deal of book knowledge. He tended to go to books for his mentoring. Best to go to the source, but few humans knew how to do that at this time. She could work with him.

As Wren arrived at the spot where Juanita had rested the exquisite branch, Wren recognized its potential immediately. He sat down, leaning against her poplar tree home without realizing anyone was there. She would have to use a little magic to get his attention. Inside the tree, she started humming, aiming her breath at the other side of the "wall" he was leaning against. She hummed a sweet lullaby at first, deepening the tones as she went along so that he would enter a light trance state.

Once he seemed to be napping, she went outside with her carving knives and a sample stick and began to make a demonstration. She did her best to tune into his ideas as much as she could find them in his consciousness. But, she also expanded upon a few. She had her own sense of beauty and could not leave that unattended.

	She continued humming while she worked because her demonstration would find its way into Wren's mind more easily if it were riding on a melody. She discovered, in his consciousness, that there were stories there and songs and dances and prayers and many, many fine nature experiences. This made her sing all the more happily. When her carving was finished, she held the finely-crafted stick straight up before his closed eyes. "There," she said, "Let this be your inspiration and your lesson. I am sure you will do a good job." And she went back into the house to finish her tea and take a little nap herself.

Manhood

  Andret called Reuban to say that he would be a little late getting to the farm today. He wanted to stay with Arjana to see what would come next in this amazing new twist of his life. He asked Arjana, "What do you like for breakfast? And what is your usual day, I mean, do you work or anything?"
  "I eat whatever is left in the refrigerator, usually. I am out of work right now, but I can do anything, anything hard, like dig ditches all day."
  "In that case, I think I can get you immediate employment. I work at an organic farm, and Reuban, my boss, has a long list of chores before winter sets in. He could use some help, if you want to work that is."
  "Andret, you probably think I am good for nothing. I mean, you probably think I have no goals, no hopes, no skills. Just a lost soul. But, I assure you, I am not."
  "No, no, I did not mean to imply that. I am just curious, since I do not know anything about you, what your average day is like, what your interests are, things like that," said Andret.
  "I walk. I often walk around town. Sometimes I go out into the country. I look at things. Then, I come home and I paint them," said Arjana.
  "May I see some of your paintings?"
  "Yes. They are in the pantry. I'll get them." Arjana opened the pantry door. There were a few cans of food, some miscellaneous kitchen items and stacks of paper, all paintings.
"I have not shown them or tried to sell them. Sometimes I give some away. I am still learning."
  "Arjana, these are great! The colors are blazing, jumping off the page, yet there is a sensitivity here as well. You seem to have an eye for intricate, small details. I would love to show these to my friend, Shae. She is also a painter."
  "Maybe, but not today. Today, I would like to paint you. Are you free?"

"I can be, yes. I have until the afternoon or I can call Reuban and tell him that I will be there tomorrow."

"No, this morning will do. Just go about making breakfast. My sister gave me some eggs yesterday. I will paint while you cook."

"So, you have family nearby?" asked Andret.

"Not really. She drove from several hours away. She knew I had been out of work for awhile, and she was being kind. Her neighbor has some chickens and gives her the extras. She lives near Chicago. That is where the rest of my family is. I moved because life was very hard there. Poverty was making all of my friends either crazy or violent. Some crazy with drugs. Some crazy with stealing. Some just born crazy. Some good, but crazy confused. I had to get out.

"I took whatever job I could find, usually hard labor, and made my way this far. I like Bloomington. It is small, but feels relatively safe, at least until last night. I hope I am not dragging the craziness with me. Things like that used to happen every day in my neighborhood."

"Sounds like you could learn some things about that, about dragging your past with you, from a friend I have called Grandmother. She teaches a small group of people who are now my friends. I actually met them there at her class. She is dedicated to helping anyone who sincerely wants to change their life and is willing to do the work.

"The past tends to hang onto us until we put some work into letting it go. She has been helping me to see that I have tended to let everyone else take charge of my life, afraid to take control of it myself. Last night, I took charge. And this morning I feel like a new person," said Andret.

"That sounds good. I would like to meet her." Arjana was already sketching.

"It is interesting feeling your eyes on me, your attention. It is like you are caressing me with your eyes."

"How could I be otherwise. You have given me the gift of

yourself and the gift of myself. I want to record every color in your skin, every curve of your muscle. I want the picture to radiate the qualities I felt in your body. I don't want any of the memory to fly away from me. Ever."

"The eggs are ready, would you like anything else?"

"Stop. Look at me," said Arjana. "Do not be afraid. I am your friend. I will never hurt you."

Andret was afraid, but he was also very brave. His bravery of last night assured him that it was worth getting over whatever fears he still held. The intensity of last night opened some part of him that now was trying to put itself back in the closet. Why? There were a million reasons, he thought, but discarded them all.

"I am sorry, Arjana. My fear is that if I continue to reveal myself, my real self to you, you will reject me. I will be hurt. I will run and hide. I am sorry. I do not want to be afraid. Can you help me not to be afraid, Arjana?"

"I can. Let me feed you these eggs. No, I am not kidding. I think we have to go back to when we were babies, to redo our childhood, all those things our mothers or fathers did not do well. It is like when you bathed me last night and when you held me in the alley. Holding close, bathing, rocking, maybe singing lullabies to each other. Maybe playing baseball or skating or bicycling. Who knows? I know that all of those things were missing from my life and you began to supply them. It only took one night, and I feel like years of my life have been replaced.

"You sit there, let me feed you. You are everything to me." Arjana picked up the fork and very ceremoniously brought it to the lips of Andret who closed his eyes and accepted this re-doing. It was then as if he had never tasted an egg before. Never one as delicious as this one. Never one that felt truly like communion with a Divine Being. He did not want to open his eyes, to spoil the image arising in his consciousness. This was, indeed, God feeding him at this moment.

It took a long time, a purposely long time. Every mouthful

was as sensuous as it could be. Andret's taste buds had never felt so alive. An egg. An ordinary egg. A beginning. The shell of Andret's life had been broken through. What better symbol of this new phase of life.

"Let me feed you now, Arjana." And the ritual was repeated. Arjana tasted again the deep caring that emanated from Andret. He kept his eyes open, not wanting to miss the movement, the color, the changing lines of what would become a painting of Andret. He studied just how Andret lifted the fork, how his fingers looked holding the stem. How his face became calm.

"I would have wanted you as my father," said Arjana. "I did not know my father at all. He was not there."

"I'm sorry," said Andret. "I did have a father at home, but he was not there either."

"We can be fathers...and brothers...and...what shall we call ourselves?" asked Arjana.

"Men," said Arjana. "Let us call ourselves men."

On the Way

The next day, Andret assured Arjana that he would come back at supper time, bring food, and their lives would continue to unfold together. Arjana had some fear that this would not be so, not because he did not believe Andret, but because of his whole life history of abandonment. But, he said, "Good. I will be here."

On the way to Reuban's garden, Andret stopped at his own apartment to change clothes and freshen up. He decided that he had time to stop by Shae's and tell her the news. They had been friends a long time and he knew that she wished that he would find a good partner for himself. She would be happy.

"Shae! I have news. I am in love."
"Oh, Andret, how wonderful! Tell me all about it."
"Well, it is a very strange story..." Andret began and related as much as he could about the events that had taken place. He tried to express the deep meaning everything had for him, but realized how inadequate his words were compared to the actual experience. "I have never experienced anything like this before, Shae. I think I may have to write a song about it or a poem or something because it goes way beyond what I have said to you."

"I think I know, Andret. I could always see some enchanted being inside of you, someone so delicate and fair that if he came out from the woods he would be annihilated by the sheer force of the world. Yet, you have also shown your strengths and commitment to your friends and to working with the land. You are not at all a weak person, more like an angel or some kind of forest spirit. I am so glad that you have found someone who recognizes you and has brought these qualities to the surface. I am sure we will all enjoy them even more." Shae hugged Andret and let him go off to work.

"Reuban, I am a new man this morning." Reuban stood back and gave Andret a once-over look. "Yes, I can see that you are," he said.

"You seem a bit taller, more filled out. Your cheeks have a bit of a tint. Tell me more," said Reuban.

"I saved someone's life last night. And he turned out to be a most wonderful fellow. I will tell you more as we work."

"Fair enough," said Reuban. They worked side by side harvesting the last of the tomatoes and squash and continuing to clean the garden tools and get things ready for storage over the winter.

"Life is like this," said Reuban. "You ripen for a long time, then all of sudden, or so it seems, you are just at the perfect stage of plump juiciness and someone picks you," he laughed. "This is your stage of deliciousness. You could store yourself for later consumption, but I recommend that you enjoy yourself right now, fully and completely."

"Thanks Reuban. I have watched you and your family over the years and hope that I can make some kind of situation that is similar, that is compatible and ongoing, everyone continuing to love each other as we grow and change."

"I think you will do it, Andret. You have what it takes. Follow the feelings you are having right now. They are strong and real. Don't let them down. When I met Kate-Amee, she was singing a song that spoke the exact feelings I was holding in my heart. I did not waste a second. I went right up to her on stage and introduced myself. I have never regretted it. Never let a good inclination pass without acting."

The Staff

Being held in Wren's hand felt to the branch of maple that it was about to be put into the service of a king. Juanita had often recited stories to the forest beings about the importance of wood in the lives of all the ancient ones. She had said that long ago, only fine craftsmen handled wood to make things for the royal family, and the peasantry very carefully chose wood for their purposes so that it would last a long time. "She made us feel very important."

"Wren's hand is the hand of a craftsman. He has a strong grip and his thoughts are moving deep into my heartwood. I am to become a staff for a young man beginning his quest to reach the peaks of his life existence. I will be the central focus in a ceremony now being designed by a group of elders. I am to hold their intentions and their wisdom throughout the life of this young man and bring him courage when he is in need," thought the branch.

All the forest listened to the story the branch was telling as it was carried along. Rumors spread quickly from tree to tree, birds listening, squirrels taking note, even the chipmunks paying attention. By the time Wren got to his van, the Faer Folk had gathered round to bid farewell to the branch and the Little People had brought a few gifts. The branch itself was, of course, Juanita's gift, and she had imbued it with proper instructions. A tanned leather strip with an eagle feather was tied to Wren's rearview side mirror, a gift from the menfolk. EC had chiseled out the letters C-A-R-L-O-S from an old license plate and strung them together at the other end of the strip.

When Wren returned to his van to go home, he noticed the feathered strip with its letters and beads handing from his mirror. He was surprised by this addition to his van, but welcomed the magic at hand. The branch was pleased and sent one last message to his own kin knowing that soon he would be transformed. He was proud of his shape, grain and color and knew that he would be an excellent Ceremonial Staff. He would dedicate himself to the well-being of the boy to whom he would be presented, and his own life would be fulfilled.

Day by Day

Yaro lay in bed holding Saffi. "We must continue to be aware of our son Bryn's new journey and treat it just the same as if he has gone off on a vision quest or is adventuring like so many other young people right now, off to see the world. And the world he is exploring is even more magnificent than the one he left behind. I am not saying that we should not miss him, but that we should be glad for him. Be the parents we always have been."

"You are right, Yaro. I just cannot help crying every now and then. There was so much more I wanted to do for him and with him as he grew up."

"I know. But, he would want us to give these gifts to other children, would he not? You know how generous he was. And there are plenty of other children in the world, plenty who need anything we can give them," said Yaro.

"Soon, the men will be giving Carlos a ceremony to help him make the transition from childhood to adulthood in the big world. Perhaps we can do more to help him as he goes along. This final period of the duality can be quite challenging as the polarization intensifies.

"As the fuel supplies that we once counted on to last forever diminish, more wars are going on than ever before. But we know that giant steps have been taken by those who love the planet as a living entity and work daily to correct some insult to her being. Think of all the attitudes that have shifted in our lifetime. So many more people understand now that skin color, sexual orientation, religious views, and nationalities make little difference in terms of someone's worthiness.

"These attitudes are threatened, of course, by those who still hold onto their fears, but that will be ending. We have kept the vision of a harmonious world thus far in our lives; no use letting ourselves be in fear about loneliness or loss. We have met numerous Divine Beings; why would we not meet Bryn in his ascended form?"

"Think of when we met, Saffi. There is some much greater force in charge of everything. Have we not seen that over and over again? Just as I knew back then when I was attempting to move away from the commune in Illinois with Reuban and Kate-Amee, I had to jump out of the truck and run back to you. That had not been my thought at all. I figured I would miss you, but that it would be like all the other people I had befriended and left behind. But, the farther away I got, the more it felt like my soul was being torn in half.

"We have to stay with Bryn even though the culture tells us that time will have us just get used to the fact that he is gone. I think, no, that is wrong. We must accompany him on this journey. Stay tuned to what he is doing. Meditate. Ask that he share whatever is appropriate from his level of being. Learn from him. Imagine, Saffi, we have a friend in the Great Land," Yaro smiled, "One whom we know loves us totally."

Suddenly the whole house seemed again like "home."

"Yaro, let's go outside and make an offering to the swing and bicycle and things Bryn used to enjoy. He doesn't need them now. Let's just thank them for serving him and give them away to another child. Let's let go and move on, move on not without Bryn, but with him. He too has taken his step into manhood."

Branching Out

Carlos lay on his bed staring at the ceiling sky. His room is filled with inventions, drawings, pencils, music equipment, a guitar, and books about building, adventuring and history. He wants to go somewhere, see how other parts of the world work, how different their cities are and what causes them to be that way. He knows that other cultures live by different rules entirely. What might that be like?

Here, he is expected to get some kind of job or start his own business, make as much money as possible, then what...spend it? It makes little sense to him. He wants to just continue researching his interests and inventing better ways to do everything. He knows the life histories of other inventors and explorers. Take off into fresh territory, make your own kind of life; this is appealing. He conjures images of himself taking his knife, pencils, drawing journal, snacks, maybe an axe and hammer, going to a far off wilderness, maybe with a dog or a donkey, living by his wits for a year, learning a new language, stretching his mind, giving his body a chance to become confident in its independence.

Then, Aron comes into the room. "Hey, Carlos, Dayo is making cookies, want to help?" Not quite the adventure Carlos was dreaming of, but..."Okay, just a sec," Carlos answers.

Dayo loves the feeling in the kitchen, the gooey texture of the dough, the smell of something baking, and the taste of a hot, sweet cookie. He knows his brothers will do just about anything to get him to cook for them, and he enjoys this momentary power. It is not always that the youngest gets the full approval of his older brothers.

"How many are you making, Dayo? Can we have some?"

"Well, if you help me make my cookbook I am working on when we are done," he bargained. I need some drawings. I have twenty recipes so far. I need illustrations. Mom said that I can sell them at Farmers' Market next spring."

"Anything for cookies," said Carlos.

"Hey, I'll help you package them when you go to Farmers' Market," said Aron.

Nourishment rose from the kitchen as easily as bread rising. The activities of people and the purpose of each set of tools, whether baking, drawing, making music, inventing, sleeping, bathing, basking in the sun or reading by the fire, were all synchronized. The house was a living, breathing entity coordinating all its rooms with the needs of the humans dwelling there. There was no excess and no lack, just responsiveness to the needs of the times.

The kitchen recalled a lifetime of experiences in which the smells of cinnamon and sweet breads filled the air and softened the feelings of everyone present. The stove prided itself on its precision in regulating temperatures and felt that it had something to do with the regulation of temperaments as well. All of the small appliances felt that they had a proper place to call their own, just like each person in the household.

Hartford had designed the walls to feel like strong arms enveloping the life within. The roof was sheltering like a doting grandparent. Windows opened to views which looked both at the private garden in back and the public walkway in front, allowing for moods of both time-to-oneself and invitation-to-enter the shared world. He understood that architecture, like music, could touch the deep soul and designed the house for this purpose.

Now, he is assessing the principles of temple-building, a structure expressing stability at its core, unfolding from intimate spaces to a vast expansive feeling in its vaulted ceilings, and a warm, radiant center. It must feel as welcoming as home and also encourage continuous upliftment. A temple is the people's highest values made "flesh."

The Sweat Lodge

All of the men had some time to think further on the ritual they were planning for Carlos. Wren had asked them to supply ideas for symbols to be carved onto the maple wood staff. Ayotunde was in charge of providing the instruments that would give everyone a chance to participate. Reuban was bringing the foods they would share. Hartford volunteered to be the clean-up "crew." Roan would guide the ceremony. Yaro planned to make a fire circle and was bringing a special stone from Saffi's collection to be an offering from the women.

The stone, an open geode showing its crystal interior dug from local ground, had been passed to all the women who then placed their love into it and made prayers that Carlos would continue to hold the Earth in high regard and, thereby, be blessed by it. They also affirmed that it would remind him of his place here on this local ground and in their very local hearts.

Stefan and Andret decided to build a sweat lodge based on the native structures that Stefan had observed in his childhood. The lodge would be at Reuban's farm out of sight of the house and barns. Noshi and Aiyana had taught the traditional sweat lodge practices to many of the group, and they had all taken part in prior ceremonies.

Andret approached the men to inquire as to whether Arjana could be a part of this ritual. He explained, "I have become very involved with Arjana and believe he would feel so honored to be a part of this important ceremony. He feels as though he has just become a man himself. And, I must say that I feel that I have just become a man because of him. I want very much for you to meet him and welcome him if you are open to that possibility."

The only hesitation was that this ceremony was to be focused on Carlos and the men could not give a new person the proper attention. After much discussion. it was agreed that a casual social gathering would be arranged as a first meeting before the ritual took place. Andret was pleased.

Taking Command

Andret did not wait for others to do the planning of this social event to welcome Arjana. He went first to Kate-Amee to get her advice on how to make it special. She had done numerous birthday celebrations, thanksgivings and holiday dinners and knew how to bring out the festive air.

He offered to pay Nola for some of her wondrous baked goods, asked Yaro if they might go fishing together to catch the main course, and made sure that Grandmother was available to come on the date he had in mind.

"Arjana," he said when he returned to Arjana's apartment, "I have arranged a dinner with all of my friends so that we can welcome you as our guest of honor. Just pretend it is your birthday so that you don't feel embarrassed. Everyone is excited to meet you."

"Oh my god, Andret. Am I going to be acceptable? Will you help me know whatever I should know in order for them to be pleased with me?"

"No problem. They will be pleased. But, yes, I will fill you in. You should wear that blue shirt with your best pants...let me see...not these...not these...these! Oh, and this vest would look great. Do you have something besides these work boots? Maybe they are okay if I clean them up a bit. Arjana's closet was not stuffed with good choices. He had traveled light, carried mostly work clothes, spent little money on himself.

Andret enjoyed clothes, often found very fine offerings at the thrift store and sometimes embellished them himself. He loved color and style, but was often afraid to wear anything he felt might look flamboyant in public. His own apartment, however, was decorated with tapestries, teapots, luxuriously patterned chairs and tablecloths. He had met Grandmother at a fabric show and admired her art quilts. They had talked a long time about how fabric is something which constantly surrounds us and, therefore, should give us ultimate comfort.

He had been a little afraid to invite Arjana into his personal domain. The difference in their apartment decor could not have been more extreme. Arjana had not pressed the issue. The fact that Andret was willing to come to his humble place was good enough. Yet, by the nature of Arjana's art, Andret realized that his colorful apartment might not scare him after all.

"Arjana, I want you to come over to my place. It is time you see this side of me. Will you be my guest?"

"Andret, only if you carry me over the threshold," he laughed.

They felt more comfortable with each other every day, as if they had always been fathers...brothers...men. They made peanut butter sandwiches, drank orange juice, shared a donut for dessert. "I think we can improve upon this diet," said Andret. "All of my friends are big time into natural, wholesome, organic food. It is the foundation of health. Although, you look healthy, so I am not trying to make this an issue. I accept where you are."

"Do not offend me. I take what is given, whether that is from a dumpster or a special occasion party in my honor," said Arjana.

"I am sorry, Arjana," I did not mean to offend you. I am offering my perspective and letting you know my friends' way of life. Please forgive me."

They stopped everything. Looked at each other eye to eye again. Arjana took Andret's hand. Then he laughed. "You are being my father. Okay. I accept. I forgot that we are all things to each other. You are caring for me. You are a father. I shall be a father to you at another time. Thank you for caring for me, my father."

Andret accepted this statement. He had not intended to be a father, but it was true, he did feel like a father in this instance. "Okay, I am finished being your father for this evening. Now, I am simply Andret, your friend."

"Andret...my friend." They continued their dinner and reported on their activities of the day.

"Tomorrow, I want you to come home with me, Arjana. See how it feels in my environment. See if you like it. Will you do that?"

"Yes, I will come. You are making a good world for me. I would like to make this world together...good for both of us," said Arjana.

Night found them equal in strength and passion, equal in desire, equal in sensitivity. Night found them equally able to enjoy humility and bravado, equally able to speak and to be silent, equally able to be as children and as men.

In the coolness of the morning air, Andret said, "Get up. It is warmer at my house. Let's go."

Arjana laughed at the certainty in his friend's voice. "You are a man, Andret. We are men," said Arjana.

It seemed to them that no one had ever recognized this obvious fact before. They had been treated as children, as students, as workers, as targets for attack, as invisible, as unusual, as the wrong color, the wrong body type, the outsider, the person from a broken home, but never as just "men." They had to say it over and over to themselves.

Arjana was loving Andret's confidence. Andret was loving his own new sense of confidence. Arjana was loving being accepted totally, body and soul. Andret was leading them to his home where the idea of total acceptance would be given one more test.

Banquet of Feeling

"Explosion!" said Arjana. "Fantastic! Color! Pattern! Everywhere!" You are my painting. It is as if I am inside one of my paintings. I am home!"

Andret could not have been more pleased. "I don't bring anyone here. I just collect the most intricate and beautiful things that I come across, things that will complement everything I own, bring out the best in all that is already here. These things are my secret family. Each one has a false memory I have given it. I pretend that this was my Grandmother's chair, that she rocked me to sleep in it. I imagine that this was my father's pipe which he smoked after dinner. That my mother embroidered this tablecloth and made it especially for my birthday..."

Andret began to speak too fast. Something was coming up from deep inside. Arjana said, "Stop Andret. Come to this chair where I can hold you. Now, I am the father. You are my son. I have loved you since the day you were born." Arjana began to spontaneously make up a story, a very good story. "We can live by whatever story we tell ourselves, Andret. We will make it up together. Heal all the wounds. I love you, my son."

Andret cried. Arjana rocked him. Kept telling the story. Spoke in the fatherly tones he had heard in the best of movies. Took all the time they both needed.

By lunch time, they were outside the need for the story. They had emerged from the pages of the book of their lives. "Andret, what is for lunch?" said Arjana.

"Let's see," said Andret. At the refrigerator, Andret began tossing salad fixings to Arjana. "Catch!"

"Lettuce, cucumber, avocado, carrot, dried cranberries, pecans, mango dressing, bread, Swiss cheese, mayonnaise...on to the cabinets. Whole wheat crackers, can of chili. That should probably do it.

"I have reconsidered. You may teach me about food now.

This looks very good," said Arjana. Andret directed Arjana in the preparations, both of them enjoying the process. Again, they had easily coasted through potentially difficult emotional scenarios, as comfortable with treating each other as father and son as friends and as lovers. They were not afraid of color, not afraid of austerity, not afraid of who they really are. Fully men.

Party of Welcome

"I'm going to have your party here, Arjana. I am not going to hide out anymore. Everyone thinks I have a very small place, too humble to be welcoming. It is somewhat small, but it is not so humble. I want your paintings on the wall. I want to introduce us in the fullness of who we truly are," said Andret.

"We shall do it," replied Arjana. They cleaned, rearranged, hung pictures, went shopping for celebratory foods, made napkin holders - yes, it just happened - chose the best tablecloth, set the table with very fine dishes.

"Frame the plates, Arjana. You know, put them on a placemat that harmonizes with the tablecloth. Place the napkins and silver to the sides. Pretend you are framing a picture. Make it look as good."

Arjana slowed down, rearranged his thinking into artist-mode. Looked through the drawers for just the right colors to show off the dishes and make the table vibrate with life. He found a basket, piled some fruit carefully in a complimentary scheme. Centered it on the table. "How is that?"

"Perfect!" said Andret. "Absolutely perfect," he thought. So very, very absolutely perfect.

Hartford and Nola arrived early. They instantly admired the house and began complimenting Andret and Arjana on the exquisite placement of things. Kate-Amee and Reuban entered with a basket of harvest vegetables, hugging Arjana as if he were already a part of the family. Ayotunde came singing through the doorway, introduced himself to Arjana and said, "You have brought joy to my friend, Andret. I can only love you." Keara placed one of her hoya plants in Arjana's hands and said, "May it bless your life with its fragrance."

Wren offered his hand, then gave Arjana a full hug of acceptance. Shae said, "I am so pleased to meet you. I want to know everything about you." Arjana blushed. Roan, Saffi and

Yaro greeted Arjana with affection and remarked on the beauty of the room. Tsura and Stefan came with hearts full of blessings and bottles of sparkling cranberry juice.

Everyone wanted a tour of the apartment with explanations of why Andret had never invited them there before. They joked and laughed and tasted the lightness in the hearts of Andret and Arjana. They spoke of paintings and cloth, of gardens and schools, of children and buildings, of cities and wilderness. They gleaned what they could of Arjana's life before Bloomington, not wanting to pry into a past that seemed unfit for anyone to have lived.

"A city needs to be a place where a small boy, as he walks through it, may see something that will tell him what he wants to do with his whole life," said Hartford. "That is a quote from architect Louis Kahn. I wholeheartedly believe this. Our cities have become places of alienation. They separate us rather than draw us together. How they are constructed makes so much difference. Locally, we are attempting to reconstruct a city which is human-friendly, not just a place for cars to drive through, but a place with its own spirit. I hope you find it welcoming to you, Arjana."

"I don't quite know what to say. I feel very welcome here since I have met Andret and all of you. But, it took an unfortunate incident to bring this all about."

"I hope we can make up for that, Arjana. Crime does happen sometimes. It is not a perfect place. But, there are many, many good people here who are working to correct all the problems we see. I would bet there are a hundred humanitarian organizations here, doing everything from feeding the hungry to sheltering victims of domestic violence. And more," said Wren.

"This is very heartening," said Arjana. "I wish I had grown up here. However, I feel that I have grown immensely in the last few days."

"Bring on the cake," said Andret as he came out of the kitchen with a scrumptious, decorated cake with one candle on it. I had Nola make this masterpiece to celebrate the first gathering of all my friends at my home and the first occasion of sharing my whole life with Arjana. Let's sing Happy Birthday because we have been reborn."

It was hard to tell whether the radiance came from the cake, the candle, the people, the paintings or the room. Everything complimented everything else. There was nothing in the room without personal meaning, not a piece of cloth, nor a color, nor a delicacy. To say that the table was happy would be such an understatement. It was made for this!
Every item that Andret had collected was made for celebrating. Long-stemmed goblets. Silver spoons. Hand-painted china. A wedding ring quilt. Valentines. A trophy. A Tiffany lamp. A circus painting. A boy scout medal. The candle on the cake. Recently added were Arjana's paintings: "The Shoulder of a Woman," "One Fallen Leaf," "The Looking Glass," "Incident in the Alley," "Hand on the Pan," "The Feeding," "Moment of Rapture." All studies of small parts of life ... parts of aliveness ... things that brought the feeling of aliveness into Arjana's body.

As time eventually summoned everyone to head for home, a sleepy wonder hovered in the room. How had things become so different than they had been just weeks ago? What brought out these expressions of even deeper layers of love? How had the courage to reveal one's intimate exaltations with others taken over? Is the Golden Age really upon us? Questions drifted through the group mind, pausing at individual doorsteps to knock and see if anyone was up for opening the door a little further. And a little further.

Initiation Day

Just before dawn the men gathered at the sweat lodge prepared the day before on the hill overlooking Reuban and Kate-Amee's pond. Clothes were hung over the limbs of trees. A fire was burning to heat the rocks. Andret and Arjana had volunteered to be the firekeepers and would use pitchforks to bring the hot stones into the domed lodge structure as needed.

Hartford, Reuban, Yaro, Wren, Ayotunde, Stefan, Carlos and Roan entered, leaving space for Andret and Arjana to enter and sit near the low flap opening. Roan poured water on the rocks to make them steam. The hotter the lodge, the more focused the attention. It was not easy for those who were older or not used to it to sit crosslegged on the ground without back support. The lodge was not about comfort. It was about intention, will and the desire to communicate with the sacred realm.

The heat and the ritual brought out whatever was in need of healing and release, from body toxins to emotional pain. It was the leader Roan's job to attune to just how much heat to create and to guide the prayer rounds and the chanting. All were naked as in the womb of Mother Earth and were expected to take off the layers of life that covered their hearts and souls as well.

It was completely dark inside the lodge, so a Talking Stick was passed from one man to the next around the circle to give each one a chance to speak. Hartford said, "Great Spirit who has guided us here this day, we welcome you. Our ceremony is in behalf of our son, Carlos, who is of the age of becoming a man. It is not a physical age as much as an age of emotional and spiritual maturity. He will be assuming many responsibilities in this world very soon, and we wish him to be well-prepared to meet his challenges. We pray that you will see the beauty of his soul and help him through all crossings. Ho."

"Great Spirit, I am Reuban. I pray that Carlos will continue to learn from the Earth herself, to join forces with the land to create food for himself and those he loves, to find time to enjoy his creative pursuits, and to bring his works to his community. I pledge my help and support in these matters. Ho."

"Yaro here, Great Spirit. My son Bryn has recently come into your realm. Now, I am pledging my support to this young man Carlos who sits with us in the men's lodge. Help me to love my son Bryn by loving our son Carlos. Strengthen me in my commitment to move beyond grief and to find enrichment in this portion of my Earth life. Thank you. Ho."

"I am Wren, Great Spirit. My prayer is that I continue to be open to learning everything I can about fathering, about nurturing others, without the need of bringing another child into an overburdened world. I send my thanks to you for the opportunity to be among these fine men who share this lodge with me and to be a part of this ceremony for Carlos. I am at your service. Ho."

"I am called Ayotunde. My name has given my life meaning. I am a bringer of joy. The name Carlos means "man." I pray that you will help Carlos to live his life in the way that you designed man to live, that you will help him to be strong, courageous, inventive and at the same time nurturing, tender and intimate with You. I pray he will know his part in Creation, find his voice, speak from his power. Make him a true Man of Love, My Creator. This is my prayer. Ho."

"I am Stefan. Great Beings who watch over us, I ask that you continue to embrace Carlos with your love and guide him to his highest path of life. Ho."

"Great Spirit, I am Carlos. I am thankful to be here with my friends and father. I am open to your help and guidance through my life. I would like to help others and to explore your Earth, and I would like to create things that will help humankind. Ho."

"I am Roan. Holy Ones, please be with us throughout this ceremony and throughout our lives. We have been extremely blessed by your Presence. For this we are deeply grateful. I ask that you would continue to assist Carlos in realizing your presence within his own being and help him to understand how to use the many talents and skills you have given to him. Ho."

"I am Andret, Great Spirit. I would like to express my happiness and gratitude for the gift of Arjana and the gift of myself which I feel I have just discovered. May our friend, Carlos, also find his true self and have the courage to bring it forth. Ho."

"I am Arjana. God, Great Spirit, Knower of All Things, you have filled my heart. I am thankful. Please fill the hearts of all of my friends gathered here. Please bring Carlos gracefully into his manhood. Ho."

More water was poured on the rocks and chants were sung. The darkness allowed the men to forget their physical separation from each other and to attend to the common prayer spoken by all of the voices. The sweat lodge womb would now generate the birth of all of their intentions and propel them into the field of life.

Another round of prayers were spoken, giving each a chance to bring up anything which had arisen within them while others were speaking. Again, the rocks were blessed with water and steam filled the hot air. Chants were continued. At this time, anyone could leave the lodge or choose to remain for another round. Several chose to exit, feeling complete. Some stayed to experience a deeper sense of cleansing themselves or clearing their consciousness from other thoughts.

When everyone entered the daylight again, some took a quick dip in the very cold pond nearby. For a few moments, a very hot body does not experience the icy coldness of the water. It was a thrill. Then the men retreated quickly to the fire where they stood naked, having revealed themselves fully to Carlos as an acknowledgement of their own vulnerability to life which does not concern itself with age or skill. Life takes what it needs from us, and if we take what we need from life, it will be good.

When sufficiently warmed, they dressed and added wood to the campfire. Andret and Arjana set up the cooking rack atop the rocks and brought out cups and pans and a crock of water for coffee or tea. They made eggs and biscuits for their breakfast and allowed some time for casual conversation before beginning the next phase of the ritual.

Watching the men around the fire, the forest remembered the gathering of many tribal people on the land. It heard the ancient voices singing, felt the laughter and the pain. Memories are stored in every tree and rock and in the earth itself. They began to be released into the consciousness of this new band of men now returning to the old ways. Deep in the bones of each man, a warrior still lives. Times have changed the costumes and the spoken language, but the language of the heart remains.

Carlos began to get a sense of how it might have been long ago when the young men walked with the elders each day to hunt and fish and gather. How it might have been to ride the ponies, carve the arrowheads, shoot the bow. He knew he was not like these tribal people in so many ways, but still he longed for just a little more of their freedom. The freedom to feel their bodies as an integral part of nature, to put their total energy toward searching or running or riding.

He knew this feeling of at-one-ment when he could devote his time to any of his creative pursuits, but he did not feel it at the computer or at the grocery store or at the public school he had once attended. He knew that many boys and men almost never felt it. He was not willing to live without this feeling. "I am going to give myself fully to everything I do," he said abruptly without thinking.

"Excellent, Carlos," said Wren. "Excellent."

Catching the Balls

A circle was made around Carlos. The toss began with Roan. "Here is a challenge I toss to you. Will you take care of your body and assure its good health?"

"Yes," said Carlos as he caught the ball.

"Will you care for the Earth in a place you call home?" asked Wren as he tossed the next ball.

"Yes," said Carlos as he caught the ball.

"Will you sing? I want to hear you sing right now. Sing any words that come from inside yourself. I must hear your voice strong and clear for it will be required of you in so many ways," said Ayotunde as he threw another ball.

Carlos hesitated, did not catch the ball. He knew that this meant he would get another chance later.

"Will you take the hand of a child younger than yourself and teach him kindly what you have learned?" asked Reuban.

"Yes," said Carlos as he caught the ball.

"Can you deal with death, and how shall you do so?" asked Yaro.

Again, Carlos hesitated and missed the ball.

Stefan said, "Carlos, will you look into the eyes of another person here and identify what they need from you?"

Quickly, Carlos caught the ball and went over to Hartford. Looking directly into the eyes of this man who had become his father, he said, "I love you, Hartford. Thank you for making this happen for me." Hartford touched his ball to Carlos' heart. Carlos accepted it.

Andret threw his ball and asked, "Can you show us a posture or a dance or a movement that lets us know you believe in your body, that you are proud of it?"

The ball was not caught.

Arjana said, "Carlos, can you tell us exactly what you feel right now?"

Carlos caught the ball and replied, "I am frightened. I am

afraid that I have failed you because I have not caught all the balls. I am afraid to sing and show my dance, and I do not know how I will handle death."

The men said, "You have not disappointed us. You have shown us your vulnerability. This is a very important quality, and it takes bravery to show it. But, you must still show us your song and dance and way of dealing with death. We are going to leave you here by the campfire and will return in an hour to see if you are ready then. If not, we will leave again for another period of time. But, we will not abandon you." Then, they got up and left.

Carlos sat watching the flames, putting another log on the pile. He wanted so much to do something powerful, not just for the men, but for himself. All the trees were listening to his thoughts. A few crows came by. The fire sparked and crackled. The day was cold. He began to feel angry with himself, to feel a heat rising in his body, a heat of will, a heat of desire.

He called out, "I am ready!"

The men returned, sat in silence with solemn faces watching. Carlos yelled, "Death, I am not ready for you yet! Do not come. And do not take anyone from me again! Wait until I am strong. I will become strong!" He began to dance wildly, to jump and hop and turn. He continued to speak loudly and ever more firmly, to command his power. "I will love...and I will fill the day with things I love...and I will put love into everything that I do. Then, Death, you cannot surprise me. I will be ready for you. I will have fulfilled my life." And he began to sing. To sing with a stronger and stronger voice. With eyes closed, still dancing, he sang.

"I am Carlos. I am a warrior. This is my tribe! I will love them. I will create life with them! I am Carlos! I am Carlos! I am a man...becoming myself!" And he danced and danced until the men got up and joined him in the dancing. They sang too. "He is Carlos. Warrior Carlos. He is one of us. He is our son!"
And they sang this chant and danced this dance for a very long time

until the whole forest believed it, until the entire Earth knew it was true, until the sky also understood the meaning of this day. Carlos is a man.

The Presentation

They took a break and gathered more firewood and food for their next meal. It was prepared without much conversation. They did not want to diminish the power of what had just occurred. In the silence, they could continue to feel their tribalness, the conquering of Death, and the love they had for each other.

Afterwards, Wren brought forth the staff. It was exquisitely done. Polished. With feathers, stones, beads and rawhide ribbons. The men passed the staff, each saying another prayer, affirmation or comment in behalf of Carlos. It was decided that Hartford then would make the presentation.

"Carlos, you have entered my home, become my family and my friend. I give you this staff as a symbol of your power to continue carving your own life path. The strength of all of us has been placed in this staff and will always be with you. I love you." Their bodies touched and their energies blended more than they ever had before. Each aura enlarged until they felt like gods, like mythological beings who could do anything. Anything. And who also knew that there was nothing else to be done.

The Message

Arriving home again after several days at Andret's apartment, Arjana listened to his answering machine. "Monifa here. I need to talk to you. I have just found out that I am pregnant and need your advice." He tapped in her number, no answer. His mind spewed out angry thoughts, transforming into mildly irritated concerns, then into despair. He reviewed his family history of problems, inability to solve them successfully and the difficulties he encountered leaving the family patterns. He had hoped Monifa was also on her way out of these dilemmas.

He punched the numbers again. "Hello," she answered.
"Monifa, this is Arjana. Tell me what is happening."
"Arjana, really, I was using birth control, but it failed to work. I did not plan this. I'm sorry. I have been going out with Robert, my boss at the Tech Center. He is a lot of fun to be with, but I am not interested in making it more than it is. Neither is he. I have not told him yet. I may not tell him. But I need to decide how to handle this. Can I come to visit and talk with you?"
"Yes, Saturday. Many things have changed for me, Monifa. We can talk about all of this. Do not make any decisions until we talk, promise?"
"I promise."
"Just when things were picking up for me," Arjana thought. "I want to forget my old life." Old temptations flooded in. ... alcohol ... drugs ... losing himself in an intense one-nighter. "Disgusting," he reprimanded himself. He began to cry, to cry loud and alone. To cry to God and to Andret. "Don't let me forsake myself again! I have just found hope."

At that moment, the phone rang again. To the answering machine, Andret began to speak, "Arjana, you have only been gone a few hours, but I am missing you already. Come back as soon as you can. All of a sudden, I just felt..." Arjana picked up the phone.

"Andret, I am coming right over. Thank you."

Arjana bicycled as fast as he could peddle on the bike loaned to him by Andret. Focusing his physical power in this way allowed him to feel that he was leaving all the emotional sorrows behind. He stared at the road, concentrated on his breath, kept his mind filled with the love of Andret and with all of the other people he had just met, people who also know something about love. "How did they get this way?" he wondered. "How do you learn to love so completely? How can I learn? Am I learning?"

Arriving, Andret opened the door, his heart, his arms, said nothing. Arjana, out-of-breath, dissolved into the love offered to him. "What happened?" said Andret.

"My sister..." he began. Told her story, his story, the tale of all victims.

"Arjana. We will take care of her. I am sure there is a way. Come. Let's make tea and talk more. There is always a way."

The Visit

Monifa drove down from the city in her old Pontiac. She hated this car, but laughed because of all the good times she had had in it. She did love a good time. "Bruce. Robert. Charles. Who was that ... oh yeah ... Renaldo, he was a trip. But, shi... now, what am I going to do? No f......ing baby, no siree. That would definitely cramp my style. But Robert is going to be really peeved. Probably ditch me. Then, we have to f....ing work together. God............!$%#!"

Miles later, she daydreamed, "I'll just have the f.....ing baby. I'll quit the damn job. The hell with Robert. To hell with all of them. I'll just get into motherhood. Love the kid. But, how will I support myself? Shi.......ucks."

The old Pontiac had heard it all before. Monifa often went from one extreme to the other. The back seat accommodated her as best it could in all types of situations. It was roomy and wide. The driver's seat, well, it put her "in the driver's seat!" In charge of her life. She could get the heck out of town or go where she darn well pleased when she wanted to. As long as she had money. And this job gave here plenty. Well, plenty for her need to blow it on fun and still pay the rent.

She parked in front of the Victorian. Laughed again at how the big, ornate house had divided itself into crummy little apartments, kind of like she had divided herself into little pieces in order to satisfy different people wanting different things from her. She tossed her cigarette on the ground, then thought better of it, picked it up, put the butt in her purse. Shook her head and walked to the door.

"Monifa, come in," said Arjana. "I just made something called a 'smoothie.' It's good. Want to have some?"

"Smoothie, my ......," she started, but again, thought better of it and said, "my goodness. You have changed. You even look different. You get a job or somethin'?"

"Yes, I have a job working at a very small farm, helping Reuban get ready for winter. More than that, I have a new friend. You can meet him tonight if you want to. We can visit after we have talked together. Let's talk about you first. That is why you are here."

Monifa related all her escapades, the good and the bad of them, the thrills and the chills of them. They explored possible outcomes, ways to cope, ways to come out on top or at least not be buried underneath the circumstances. Their tentative plan was for Monifa to quit her job in a few weeks, move into Arjana's apartment, move Arjana into Andret's apartment, start the flow toward a new life.

"I will help in every way. I will introduce you to a group of very fine people who have helped me to feel welcome here and have shown me new ways of thinking and living. I feel very at home. They make me feel at home, the kind of home we never had."

"Are they fun?" she asked.

"Not in the ways that you are used to," said Arjana, "but you will learn new ways of enjoying life if you care to."

"I'm going to have to learn new ways of just about everything if I have this kid," she replied.

"You will learn those too," Arjana said.

In the evening, they picked up Andret in the Pontiac and went to dinner at Miss Piggy's Barbeque. Arjana did not want to force her into too many new experiences all at once. Andret had not-the-worst-he-had-ever-eaten salad. Arjana and Monifa devoured a giant, saucy pork sandwich with fries and lemonade. "It's a family tradition," said Arjana, "at least in Chicago." They all laughed and talked about food, lifestyles, habits and whether one should deny the flesh anything it wants.

"What good is life if you can't satisfy your desires?' asked Monifa.

"I am really not the one to ask," said Andret. "It is a good question though, and I know just the people who would be happy to give you answers. Maybe not the same answers, but answers nonetheless. You will meet them sometime I'm sure."

"Do you think its possible to have a fun and fulfilling life with a baby?" she asked.

"My boss and his wife, Reuban and Kate-Amee, have three children who seem to delight them constantly. My other friends, Saffi and Yaro, had a wonderful son, Bryn, who just died recently. They were totally devoted to him and seemed very happy."

"'Bryn,' I like that name," said Monifa. They continued to chatter lightheartedly about whatever came to mind. Details of the proposed plan for Monifa's life change were tossed out, tried on, rejected or accepted, throughout lemonade refills and chocolate cream pie dessert with coffee.

They drove the Pontiac back to the Victorian, made sure Monifa was comfortable and agreed to drive back in the morning before breakfast as long as that meant not before 10am. Monifa let them borrow the car for the night and said that she would behave and get a good night's rest.

The Altar

Roan left for India shortly after Carlos' ritual. The leaves were gone from the trees. The sun tended to hide behind clouds a little more often. The world...if one listened to the news...seemed to be in deadly turmoil even with so many people working to solve its problems. And, of course, Bryn was no longer physically present in Saffi and Yaro's household.

"Saffi, we have to do something. I want us to make Bryn's room a sanctuary. It will be where we meditate together each day. It will be a portal of communication with Bryn and those who dwell in the Great Land. Perhaps, it will also be a place of refuge, when needed, for guests who might require our help. Let us keep a daily journal of Bryn's communications with us and whatever else may come through our meditations. How does that sound to you?"

"I have been heading in that direction, though with less of a focus. I think you are right. I have cleared out extraneous belongings, especially those that trigger sadness. Let's move the furniture and everything and take it down to bare walls. Then, we can repaint and start afresh," said Saffi.

Over the weeks, the room divested itself of its link to "little boyness." It welcomed the wash of its walls and windows. Though it had been the place where many childhood dreams were stored, it was willing now to accept another role. The ceiling became a blue sky. Around the window, the woodwork was painted deep pink. Walls were stippled with variations of golden orange to pale yellow, as if a sunrise were occurring.

"Room of the Rising Sun!" said Yaro. That is what this shall be, the room of our rising son. They created an altar in front of the window, a low table made of found wood and a slab of marble that had once been a countertop. Everything was ceremoniously cleaned with lemon water and polished to look like new. Saffi still had the sheepskin blanket that Bryn had loved as a baby. She placed it on the floor in front of the altar.

"Yaro, let's make love. Let's conceive not another child,

but a new life for our son Bryn. We can ask the monks to open us to the Temple of Love and go to the Adoration Room to which we were once invited."

It seemed right. Because it was a ritual, they chose a time before dawn the next morning. They would awaken early, shower, dress lightly. They agreed on the accoutrements needed. They prepared the space for their comfort. They tied up loose ends of business so that there would be no chance of interruption. Yaro arranged for a substitute driver for his school bus route. Saffi finished filling the orders for her handmade journals. They made sure their minds would be at peace.

In the deep, dark morning of a crisp winter day, they entered this newly prepared sanctuary, glowing like the small heater in the corner. They sat facing each other resting as gracefully as the orchid in the slender green vase. Breathing, they became the fragrance.

Upon entering the Temple of Love in their mind's eye, they knew there were no limits on what may be given to them. They were reaching into the majesty of each other and of the God Within All Things.

"There is a love breath that tiptoes in once we let the world fall away. We find it roaming inside our bodies, searching for itself, opening cell doors and calling for the One Supreme. We want to sing and swoon and sway with this One Who Brings Forth Life. We want no barriers between this Infinite Being and our Self-in-Time.

"In the Grand Room of the Heart, we find two wine goblets waiting and begin to taste. Our lips on the rim of eternity, it takes only one sip, and we become the untarnished template of our physical body, a flawless manifestation of our loving intention to enter into the fullness of our godselves. Into this splendor, we pour ourselves as if we are liquid light.

"Consciousness slides in slow motion into touch as soft as the tender petals of the orchid flower before us. Lovemaking flows seamlessly as we explore the caress which has never been taught. There are no walls in this room. There is no passivity in this interchange. There is only a gathering-to, a welcoming-in and a giving-forth. Skilled hands massage each part of the body as if it is the most desired part, as if it is the only part. Body, mind and soul enter into supreme sensation as each petal of the flower opens.

"Kneeling, he enters the widely yawning gateway. There is a fluttering like silent wings. Rising. Circling. Hovering. I draw him down, opening. He drifts down as silently as a feather falling. The wings of delight spread open, then wrap around in warm embracing. Squeezing. Again."

"Thrusting, I am swallowed into the flower and the honey flows."

"Turning. Returning. We breathe into the flames now kindling. There is the treat of tongues. There is the sharing of sounds. Bashfulness no longer exists. Straddling, I remember the juice of a mango. I taste again. Sighing. Almost crying...with delight."

"Standing, I am the thick trunk of the tree of life. Limbs lifting to the sky. Clinging, I am the vine wrapping myself around, curling under and over this column of chi rising. Rolling. We go down. I am the Earth. All living beings make love upon my fertile ground."

"Hearts pounding. We ride astride this magical being of form which rises from the unknown, lifting its body to cast wild seed toward the creation of our intention. We are freed of all restrictions which once kept us from seeing who we truly are."

"Waves crash against us sucking out any sense of pretense. We are channels flooded with the rush of entire star systems soaring through our galaxy of love. We are everywhere God. We are everything God. We are life unbound. Poetry pours into our mouths and becomes a New World waiting only for the hand of the One Supreme to graze the surface of our flesh and bring crescendo to this rhapsody. Trembling, we come to silence."

*

    A gong sounds. Kunchen carefully lifts one of the golden chalices. "Ahhhh," he says. "Someone has tasted from this cup today." Smiling, he lifts a corner of his robe to wipe away the fingerprints of four hands.

    Suddenly, he falls to the floor, bowing to the ones who adored the God Within. A tsunami of love overpowers him and rushes past the door of the Temple of Love. The Earth below trembles, tilts and white crystals fall from the sky.

*

    Nola's hand strokes Hartford's face, her foot touches the warmth of his. "Who brought us to this place of thankfulness for each other's presence?" she wonders and also knows.

*

    Shae reaches over to Wren and kisses his shoulder. Her hands travel across the landscape of his body.
    "You are the morning itself," he informs her, knowing that if she were gone, he would not feel whole.

*

    Tsura wraps her body around Stefan and whispers, "It's happening. Another wave of divine love is traveling across the planet. Swim into it with me."

*

    Kate-Amee wakes Reuban to say, "Did you feel that?" He opens his eyes and finds the room is filled with golden light and he is in bed with the Goddess. She is captivated by his gaze.

*

    Nimi touches the moonlight now streaming in over her bed

and knows it is Bryn. "I'm waiting for you, Bryn," she says and hugs her pillow again.

*

Mirela gets out of bed and goes to the window to watch the first snow falling. Nickolas stirs in his sleep, dreaming of a crystal-filled sky.

*

Keara looks at Ayotunde, feels his full rhapsody play through her body and weeps. This is the love she wishes everyone felt. This is the love Earth needs. She reaches out and touches the leaf of one of her plants, transmitting the joy she feels. The leaf shivers and sends the energy spiraling out through the walls of the house and down to the town through all the trees and streets and buildings and down to the river Shemaya.

*

Animals lift their heads or flap their wings or crawl out from their hiding. The Little People and Faery Folk are shaken from their beds and run outside to ride on the wind.

*

Saffi and Yaro continue to tremble in the love which has overtaken them. They have lost all sense of who they are or where and know not what has happened. Their souls are carrying them through the night as simply winged delight.

*

Andret calls out to Arjana, "What is happening, my friend?" Arjana places his fingertips on the lips of Andret.
"Shhhh, it is the movement of love across the planet. I saw it in my dream. It awakened me a few moments ago and told me to hold you close."

*

The unstoppable wave continued and crashed through the walls of the Victorian house where Monifa tried to sleep. The dull beige walls of the living room suddenly turned to gold. A luminous form appeared above her and entered into her womb. It was as if the one she always wished for had finally found her there. She didn't have a name or a face for this Magnificent One, but knew the feeling when he entered and welcomed him with a scream.

*

The sound of her crying out rode the wave right on through the house and down the street where a young priest lived next door to the Catholic church. He felt the Holy Spirit had come to answer his prayers. He rose from his bed and knelt for awhile considering why he was there.

"I'm lost," he said to the God somewhere. I no longer know what I'm doing. Please help me to find my way. Show me the service you need of me. I no longer feel at home in this robe. I am dying beneath this dogma. How can I leave without causing sorrow? How can I rescind my vows and still remain your friend?"

*

The wave continued its journey traveling around the world. Each time it rolled across the land, a few more people awakened. Each time someone took the time to enter the Temple of Love in the heavens and worship their beloved, another wave rose. Each time the gong sounded in the hearts of the women and they followed its ring, the wave grew stronger. Each time the men transcended the poisons of life, the chalice in the heart was filled and some part of the Earth was healed.

*

The three monks came quickly to the side of Kunchen. They, too, bowed down. Then, they began the Prayer for the Earth they had said throughout their lives.

"Oh Cosmic Mother and Father of Creation, whose presence is known by every name, let all hearts open and all wounds be healed by this knowing. The domain of Thy kin is filled with Your glory for all things are made of Thee. All of the power and love that ever was or will be is here now and only now. Your work is done. Let us realize this fulfillment. We gratefully receive Thy bounty in accord with our ability to recognize Your presence in all that exists. The flesh of all that is alive is Your body. Thus, we cannot be separate from You nor from our good. In humility and exaltation, we bow down. Amen."

Conception

Bryn felt the release sent to him by Saffi and Yaro and allowed himself to become all that was around him in the Great Land. He floated like a golden leaf suddenly realizing its fall and noticing the brilliant colors of all of his kin now drifting on a gentle wind. He turned from heaven to earth and back again and again until caught by a blade of grass.

The Guide reached out and called the sound of the name Bryn once knew as his own. Instantly, his memories congealed and spun him into the appearance of flesh and bone with the senses of a human being. He remembered the wonder of Earth life and listened carefully to the instructions from the Guide.

"The way has been cleared for you, Bryn. Your parents have released you from attachment to your prior form. The wave of love generated by their devotion to the One Supreme has opened a channel which will allow your immediate and easy passage into Earth life once again. Saffi and Yaro are consciously opening themselves to become involved in a new chapter of your eternal existence. They have dismantled their expectations and, therefore, all limitations," said the Guide.

"You may enter the womb of a young woman who is the sister of Arjana, the person whose life you saved in the alley. Her name is Monifa. She is struggling to release herself from the constrictions of harsh circumstances and situations of violence, and she is beginning to take control of her life. As her child, you will eventually be in contact with Yaro and Saffi and the others whom you have loved.

"You will be her only child, and she will love you. You will be healthy, but face the hostility and fear that has gathered around her. This is where you will be most helpful. You have a strong countenance, and we will advise you along the way. If you do not wish to enter Monifa's womb at this time, I am certain there will be other possibilities in the very near future. Please think this over and I will return."

Before deciding, Bryn let go again into All Things and drifted through the places he once knew, taking turns at being the river Shemaya, the yellow house, the gathering of people around a fire, the sound of their songs, the foods they shared, the gardens they worked, and finally, Nimi. It was then that his soul felt, "Yes. I will return."

The Guide and the four monks came to him. "Here is the heritage we shall link to you," they said. Starting with a tribal history hundreds of years ago, they explained what each generation had discovered, lived by and fostered in their children. They said, "You will embody the genes that will carry these ancient ways forward. Your first year will be the most challenging. The love you carry within your heart will have to penetrate the emotional wounds of Monifa.

"She will be making a difficult transition from her current lifestyle and will often be confused, angry and distraught. She may not always notice your needs. But, as the Earth energies continue to shift she will become increasingly peaceful and begin to comprehend her new direction and the importance of your being in her life.

"Then, your childhood will become integrated once again with those you have loved before. Your spiritual work will be completed at that time and you will be faced with another choice. You may continue in your life making new soul contracts with those around you, or you may return to us. In either case, you shall always return to the Great Land and to us eventually. Do you wish to continue?" asked the Guide.

"I do," said Bryn, if I shall have the opportunity to meet Nimi again and to befriend her in some way."

"You shall."

Fulfillment

Nola and Hartford lay together talking of the changes in Carlos. "I see a different look in his eyes now," said Nola. "I hugged him when he came home from the ritual and he felt like a man; really, there was a difference. He seems very at peace with himself."

"I was so touched, Nola, at his expression of love for me and, then, at his total giving of himself to the ceremony. He was magnificent. I know that sounds like a big word to put on it, but, truly, he was magnificent. I feel so fulfilled these days," said Hartford.

"Children will ask everything of you. Sometimes I am stretched to my limit, but, then, they bring you some unexpected twist that opens you. They excel at something you thought they were not getting. They clean the bathroom. They make you a present. They notice you," said Nola. "You have been through this five times now, five sons. Thank you for caring about mine, taking on this task of fatherhood after you thought you were done."

"Nola, I love you. In loving them, I love you even more. I am thankful that I have had another chance to be a family man. I am trying to make up for what I was too young and inexperienced to know how to do well in my first family. Not everyone gets a second chance."

Embracing, their words trickled off the edge of night and fell into the dream basket. Their bodies rested warm in the big bed while their spirits tiptoed out to see what was happening elsewhere in the galaxy. Scenery floated by like islands each with their own sounds and sensations while the Guides steered the silent boats toward some land of learning that might be useful to their present lives.

Sometimes the dreams are clear messages, sometimes just a view of the palette of possibilities. Occasionally, they are the living out of situations that might be impossible to experience within one's current life conditions. Now and then, a dream warns or cautions, but usually the dreams only soothe or complete unfinished emotional business. It is up to the Guide and the intent of the dreamer.

    This night in the dream of each of them, Carlos appeared in full Spanish regalia.

Church Bells

Monifa fell asleep after what she thought was a dream of golden light entering the room, just attributing it to the whole new confusion she had entered into. Now, she was hearing church bells. "What the he....? Where am I? Oh yeah, Arjana's place." She cleared her groggy mind and reminded herself of her situation. "I have a baby inside me. Oh yeah. Maybe that was an angel that came to me last night to make everything alright," she smiled and started to cheer up.

"It's only 8am. Maybe I should go down to that church and confess and get clear for that baby. I wouldn't want it to suffer from anything I've done. Yeah." She put on her clothes and took a walk down the block. The church was an old building and looked like a church should look, she thought. Bricks and stone, heavy on the bottom, a tall steeple which was probably the tallest thing in town at some point in time. "Things change though," she thought. "Now, its finance and technology buildings that reach to the sky."

She opened the big wooden door, walked into the quiet space. There were a few people in the pews, some candles burning up front near the sanctuary. She looked around for the confessional. "There. Yeah. I think I can remember how to do this." Inside the confessional, she knelt down and waited for the little sliding window to be opened by the priest. It felt kind of nice to be in such a tiny safe space. "Maybe this is what its like in the womb."

"Bless me father for I have sinned," she started, "I think I have sinned just about every day for the past thirty-five years. I haven't killed anybody, but I have had one heck of a lot of promiscuous sex for all sorts of bad reasons, sometimes stealing and cheating in the bargain." Then, she couldn't help herself; she started describing all the sexual affairs, the why's and wherefore's and how it all came about and ended.

Father Thomas tried to stop her several times, but was actually somewhat fascinated by the stories. He wondered if God could really forgive this amount of wildness and whether he, himself, could be forgiven if he had but one affair someday, sometime. Was three "Our Fathers" and three "Hail Marys" going to be enough in this situation? And, "What time is it getting to be?" but he couldn't read his watch in the darkness.

    He asked Monifa if she would like some counseling. She said, "Sure." He told her to come back at 5pm and come to his office just off the front hallway. Then, he gave the blessings of forgiveness aloud for Monifa and silently for himself.

    Monifa did not stay for mass. That would be pushing her limits. She walked back to the Victorian to wait for Arjana and Andret and her Pontiac. Maybe they could go out to breakfast. There was certainly nothing worth eating at the apartment.

Prayers

Father Thomas tried very hard to keep his mind on his prayers as he said the mass that morning. But, it was as if there were two realities taking place at once. When he lifted the host, it wasn't just a white bread wafer, nor was it only Jesus Christ. It was his life. It was as if everything he had ever done was suddenly transmitted to that little round piece of bread he was holding up to the Lord. It poured out of his arms, out of his heart, out of his soul.

The right words, thankfully, came out of his mouth in order to keep anyone from knowing what was really taking place. Mass continued as it should. But his consciousness kept seeing some other reality. He had always wanted a mystical experience, but felt unworthy, thus completely blocking any such possibility. He had also entered the seminary right out of high school having had no sexual experience whatsoever.

He spent his novice year, as all novitiates do, in silence and without contact with the outside world. No radio. No TV. No news. No letters. In some ways, that was good. He enjoyed the company of several other young men in the order, and the basics of life were taken care of throughout his remaining years of study. Once he did get assigned to a parish, he felt ill-prepared for how the world had changed.

He caught up as best he could, reading voraciously, and walking around town as much as possible. He liked ministering to the nice old ladies and enjoyed the school children, but he did not have the experiences needed to wisely counsel people with complicated problems. His life in the seminary had been totally disciplined by external rules.

Now, here was a woman this morning who really wanted to change her life from wild rebellion to loving motherhood. How could he possibly help? And why was he even trying? All of these thoughts went round and round in his head all day long, alternating with fantasies of being free of his priestly restrictions and dabbling,

at least a little, in the pleasures of the flesh ...
or maybe just thinking of the pleasures of the flesh. It was almost 5 o'clock.

The Tour

When Arjana and Andret arrived in the Pontiac that same morning, Monifa explained that she had been to church and was going back at 5 o'clock to get some counseling. Arjana wondered, "What next?" but said, "Wonderful. I am sure there are helpful people there, and it will be good to get to know some of the neighbors if you are going to live here."

They discussed the details of her move, the talk going more smoothly than expected. After a late breakfast at the Co-op Cafe - they figured it was their turn for choosing the type of meal they would have - they drove around the town and out into the countryside to give Monifa a feel for the place. Without his own car, Arjana was not familiar with all of the local interesting sites.

Andret introduced them to the limestone quarries, the scenic views from the state park overlooks, the quaint small town nearby, and drove by Reuban and Kate-Amee's farm, Grandmother's house, Saffi and Yaro's place, Shae and Wren's home, and back into town past Hartford and Nola's home in the historical neighborhood ending up a Andret's apartment. By then, it was nearly 5 o'clock, and they picked up a meal - okay, it was Monifa's turn - at the Grab & Go fast food stop.

Getting back to Arjana's with only minutes to spare, Monifa wolfed down her burger in the car, got out at the church and said she would be home to Arjana's in maybe an hour or two. "Clean up the place and pack your stuff," she said jokingly, but also hoping she could make this transition as quickly as possible so that it could keep feeling good.

She liked Andret. The town was pleasant, the surrounding area quite beautiful, and now she was headed for "counseling" which she hoped would further clear the slate so that she could begin her new life. "Wonder what Father Thomas looks like in person?"

Face to Face

Father Thomas was anxiously waiting in his office. He had already spent about half an hour tidying up the place. Papers always seemed to get out of control. The housekeeper kept the dirt out, but the mailman never ceased to bring in piles of paper that all needed somewhere to go. Even though a secretary, Miss Burns, came in once a week to do whatever needed to be done that he could not accomplish himself, he always seemed to be behind.

He wasn't fond of paperwork. He preferred face-to-face visits with the parishioners, especially at their homes. Outside the rectory walls, life could be more spontaneous, at least to a certain degree. No breaking of church rules. No crossing the line into sin. He stopped himself from bogging down into resentment for these restrictions. After all, he told himself, the church maintains a comfortable home for me, pays all the bills and feeds me sufficiently well. And in about two minutes, an interesting woman is going walk through my office door.

"Hello, I'm Father Thomas, won't you come in?" he addressed the woman. His heart took one giant flip and made him feel a wee bit faint, then he managed to regain control.

"Hello, I am Monifa. I am new in town. And, well, you heard my confession, so you know all about me."

Father Thomas's face turned rosy pink and he looked away in order to regain his composure again.

"Yes, well, yes, you have come for counseling, correct?"

"It was your idea, remember?" said Monifa.

They sat for a moment, uncertain of what to say next, looking at each other, then looking away at something in the room or in the future, or in their imaginations.

"Yes, of course," Father Thomas said. "So, tell me more about your present life situation and where you are heading."

"I'm pregnant. I love sex. I'm moving here to get away from my boyfriend who doesn't know anything about this yet. I considered abortion, but then I had a dream where this ray of golden light came down from heaven and went straight into my womb. It reminded me of Mother Mary and the shock she must have felt when that angel came and gave her the word. She wasn't married either and had to get out of town before the birth. I guess she was lucky to find Joseph and he was nice enough to take charge and get them to safety." Monifa didn't mince words.

"Ahhh...yes...I suppose that was the situation at its core, but we use a little different wording," said Father Thomas.

"Yeah, my brother, Arjana, says that words make all the difference. I'm trying to learn that, but I usually just say what I think. So, what if I say I am with child, and I'm making a pilgrimage to the holy land of Bloomington guided by the kind Father Thomas and the other two wise men, Arjana and Andret?"

"That does sound better. And I would be very glad to be helpful, to be a guide, if I can be of any service whatsoever."

"Tell me about yourself," says Monifa. And Father Thomas, without further embarrassment, begins to relate his own life story to this interesting woman who has him totally mesmerized at this point. Two hours later, she says, "I told my brother that I would be back by 7 o'clock, so I should be leaving, would you like to walk back with me, it's just down the block."

Father Thomas can hardly believe he took the entire two hours talking about himself. What's more, Monifa actually listened. "Of course, I would be happy to walk you home." He put on his coat and helped her on with hers, once again getting close enough to her physically to feel enveloped in her energy field, a buzz so compelling that he just wanted to grab her and kiss her and fall to the floor and, "Oh my God," he prayed, "forgive me...on second thought, guide me. I put this into your hands."

The Sanctuary

As they reached Arjana's, they saw the note on the door. "We went to shop for a little more food. Be back before 9pm. Love, Arjana & Andret." "Why don't you come in and see the place; maybe you can help me decide how I should fix it up for my new life. I want it to be cheerful, you know," said Monifa.

"I'm not much of a decorator, I'm afraid," Father Thomas responded, "but I will come in just to become acquainted with your situation. It is part of my parish duty to visit the homes of members of the congregation."

"You don't have to be so formal," Monifa responded. "Just say, 'Okay,' and get your ass in here. I mean, just come in. Sorry, it's those words again. I'll try to behave. I should change my language, shouldn't I."

Once they were inside and the door was closed, neither of them could contain their attraction any longer. It was a grand, passionate embrace with a good, a really good, long kiss. Then, "I'm not sorry," said Father Thomas, "that is, unless you want me to be sorry. I'm very attracted to you, and I have been considering leaving the priesthood. And I see that I should. I am not a good example of what a priest should be. But, I am a good person. I don't want to offend you. Thank you for the kiss."

"I think you could use some counseling," Monifa said. "You are carrying more guilt than I am," she laughed. Let's counsel each other, how about that? Tomorrow at 5 o'clock, is that good? My place or yours?"

"Yours. Here, if that is okay," Father Thomas said.

"I will be ready for you," Monifa replied. She contemplated saying, "We can always go to confession next weekend," but she thought better of it. She was not sure how much teasing he could take. "Take a short walk through this place before you leave and see if your 'inner decorator' has any ideas" she laughed. They walked around the two rooms.

"Not really," he said, "I can only think about tomorrow."

"Well, you do that," she said, "and I will be here at 5pm."

Father Thomas left and took the long way back to his house next to the church, going around the block in the opposite direction from which they started. His fingers automatically moved from bead to bead on the rosary in his pocket. It was a way of centering himself and of requesting guidance at the same time. He would need a lot of guidance, he thought. A lot of guidance. But, others had left the Order; it can be done.

He went into the empty church instead of into his house. He just wanted to sit in the silence for a little while. The church was always a comforting place when no one was there. Just God and Father Thomas. He had always felt a friendship with God and had tried to be a good boy as a child. His favorite nun, a teacher in grade school, had encouraged him to enter the seminary. She thought he had "the calling." That made him feel very good, very special, at the time. But now he was unsure.

"What must I do, dear Father? How can I remain in your good graces? I want very much to serve you. Yet, all of these rules and expectations that have been heaped upon me no longer seem right. My soul begs for freedom. I would like to have your permission before I engage in any sexual activity...your permission...how do I get that? More and more, I feel you work from inside me rather than from far away. I feel a closeness to you, more than I have ever felt before.

"Now, this woman tempts me, but is it really 'temptation' as if to do something sinful? I do not understand this kind of sin. You have created us with this sexual longing. Why would you have done so if it were not in keeping with your ways? I do not want to break my vows to you, but these vows were made before I was of an age to know myself. I must ask your forgiveness if I break them. Lord God, heavenly Father, my request is that you will guide me clearly through this trial. Let me know the place of my feelings and the proper place of rules that oppose them. Thank you, Father."

The sanctuary light was beautifully soft coming through

the stained glass windows. Candles glimmered in the votive lights. He looked down at his cassock, touched this familiar piece of cloth with loving kindness. It had served him well, giving him a degree of status among the people he met, protecting him sometimes from their violence, other times causing a display of anger usually at the church itself. It made him feel like Jesus, at least like one of his followers, in the beginning. It was a way of recognizing the strong spiritual part of himself that went unrecognized by others. But, perhaps, he no longer needed the robe, nor the title, to stand firmly in his spirituality. He knew he loved God. He did not need to prove it to anyone else. God surely knew his heart.

    He walked home then, to the rectory. He was glad that Monifa lived, or would soon live, just down the street. He hoped she would not meet someone else before he was able to be with her fully. In the meantime, he would take what is offered. As he fell asleep, he felt at peace, a deeper peace than he had felt in a long time.

    "Your longing is the answer," a voice said in his dream.

    "What?" he said as he awakened abruptly.

    "Your longing is the answer," the voice repeated. But, he could see no one.

Preparations

Grandmother and Stefan called all of their group of close friends together. "Some of us have been meeting for quite a few years, others are relatively new to our group. However, we are all in alignment with our goal of creating a world in which love is the bottom line. This template for human behavior is being called the Temple of Love. After many years of developing our capacity to feel and express loving kindness to all and in all areas of our lives, the Higher Beings have inspired us to create an actual physical temple on the site called the Hill.

"This work has begun with our first gift to the land, the offering of Bryn's body and, therefore, his consciousness. As we know, Bryn was an exceptional young man, a very highly-evolved soul. He gave himself fully to everyone. I call his gravesite The Heart of the Beloved, for through his example we learned many ways of loving and many ways that the Great Beloved shows love to us.

"As we cross the cusp of December 21, 2012, there may be some disruption of services in our community. Grocery supplies may run out if transportation is interrupted. Knowing that stores are only able to keep two or three days supply on hand at any given time, we have stored necessary supplies. We have attempted to make our homes as self-sufficient as possible without entering into fear and hoarding. We trust that these simple precautions will get us through any difficult part of Earth's transition.

"This meeting, however, is not about the physical changes that may take place, but the emotional ones that have already begun. Waves of divine love are traveling across the planet. You can attribute these to astrological occurrences or to our prayers and intentions or simply to the grace of God or all of the above. My point is to call attention to the emotions that may be awakened in yourselves. Some of you have already experienced bursts of loving energy toward those with whom you are in relationship. You may also begin to feel these bursts with more and more people and with

the Earth itself or even with ordinary objects. Your God-consciousness is being activated. It will only get stronger. This all sounds very, very good, but here is my concern.
You may find yourself attracted to someone unexpectedly. This could become a moral dilemma if you do not understand what is taking place.

"As always, you may make the choice that you feel is appropriate for yourself. It is just that because you are already in love with your partner, you may not expect to fall in love with anyone else. All of you seem to be making mature decisions in regard to your relationships. Should any unusual circumstances occur, however, I want you to know that I am here to listen and help you through your decision-making process. Your Guiding Ones and our helpers, the four monks, are also on hand at all times. May we all enjoy this increased love frequency as much as possible and be wise enough to handle the influx of energy in the best ways we can creatively imagine."

Grandmother's words acknowledged everyone's experiences. The entire group of people over the course of meeting together had felt intense moments of transcendental love for the people they cared about. Everyone had a very strong kinship with Earth and its plant and animal beings. They recently celebrated the pairing of Andret and Arjana. They provided a life-affirming ceremony for Carlos. And they would continue to focus on the needs of the other children as they encountered new situations within the love frequency.

"Nimi will be our next young one in need of a coming-of-age ceremony said Kate-Amee. She is already such a loving being and was so close to Bryn. She seems to be handling his parting fairly well though. She is still in communication with him."

"This loving life is what we have all been working toward," said Ayotunde. "I am so glad that we have made this commitment to each other."

Grandmother responds, "Yes, and I would like us to meet

as often as we can from now through December. We need to feel the firmness and certainty of our combined love beneath us like the ground under our feet. This may be our moment of greatest potency. Hold fast, my dear ones, hold fast."

Saffi says, "Yaro and I set up Bryn's room as a potential portal not long ago and with our first ritual we were knocked off our feet! I want to say that we made love, but it was more like love made us, and what a love it was. Our bodies were overtaken by a force so incredible, we did not have to "do" anything. I can't possibly describe it."

Shae says, "I think we felt it. Or, at least we felt the wave. My appreciation for Wren and for everything in my life just keeps increasing."

"Yes. I can attest to that," replies Hartford. "I am living in deep thankfulness. It concerns me a little that I might die and lose these wondrous blessings, but, of course, I know that that is not how it works. Life goes on. I just want you all to be with me wherever I am."

"I think there is only 'here'," responds Reuban. Our consciousness shifts, and then it seems like 'there.' We know this because of meeting the four monks both in the spirit world and, later, in physical presence. Here and There are one."

Andret says, "My meeting with Arjana has been my full awakening to the love that is coming in to the planet. Nothing has ever been this good."

"I would agree wholeheartedly with that," said Arjana.

"Let's schedule weekly dinners together, meditate and talk about how we are handling the love events, shall we?" asked Stefan.

"How about Thanksgiving at our house?" asked Wren.

"We can all bring our most-loved dish," said Nola.

"And songs," said Kate-Amee. All agreed.

Grandmother led their meditation, lifting the veils which seem to separate "here" from "there." The four monks assisted.

The Guides stood by. The sea of consciousness was perceived even more clearly. Deep, healing waters. Fragrant air. A quality of light that could only be described as celestial. They came alive in this luminous world and called it The Great Land. From this land, they received ongoing gifts which they brought back to the Earth and all of its beings.

Five O'clock

Father Thomas arrived promptly at 5pm the next day. Monifa had already re-arranged the furniture, put fresh sheets on the sofa bed, changed a few lightbulbs to get the right ambiance. The whole apartment was on the alert. You could almost hear the gossip, a kind of low electronic whisper between the toaster, the clock. the radio, the refrigerator, and the coffee pot. None of the household furnishings had seen this much action in a long time.

The bathroom started hoping for another steamy night. The one living room chair was enjoying the scarf Monifa had draped over it. The side table liked its polish. And the whole living room was feeling as though this might be the start of something big.

Monifa opened the door to the man in black framed by the white snowfall. He stepped into the room of rainbows. "I brought you some chocolates," he said. "Do you like chocolate?"

"Why thank you," she said, "I certainly do. I like a variety of flavors, especially those gooey cherries with the chocolate coating. Are there any of those in there?"

"I'm not sure. It says its a mixture, so maybe so."

"Let's talk first. We'll save these until after dinner."

It was a little stiff at first...the conversation that is. "Let's get down to it," she said. "Why are you here?"

"I want to get to know you better. I only talked about myself yesterday. I want to hear your story too. Why are you here? How can I help you...if you need help that is. I mean, I want to be your friend...or whatever God wants us to be," he stumbled on.

"For starters," she said, "I would like to try one more kiss just to see if I feel the same way today that I did yesterday." She made the advance. He didn't refuse. They let it last as long as they could.

"That's good," she said. "Now, I'll tell you what I am

looking for. I need a good friend who is as steady as a rock, someone who will see me through the ups and downs of this pregnancy and help me to settle into this new place. I have to move here, fix this place up, get ready for a child. I have to find some work, make a living, and find a life that will be fitting for a mother of an excellent child. I want to be a good mother. That means I won't be able to go out to the bars every night. I won't be having men in. No wild parties. I have to settle down, but I don't want to settle into a... she almost said the "f" word again... rut."

"You're a priest. I like you. You must be stable. You seem kind. I could use your kind of kissing ... maybe every day ... or as often as possible, just to wean me gently from more athletic activities. You know what I mean?" she continued.

"I think I am getting the picture, but go on," Father Thomas replied.

"I wouldn't be against seeing what else might develop between us, but I don't want to get you in trouble. I think the kissing is necessary though. I don't think I can give up the rest if I can't even have a kiss a day. Are you open to that?"

"At this moment, it couldn't sound more perfect," he replied. "Do you do paperwork? Like secretarial, I mean?"

"Sure," she said.

"I have a part-time secretary, Miss Burns, but she is elderly and can't do as much as I would like her to. I am always behind in my paperwork. Perhaps you could work for me in my office. I would pay you, of course. How much money will you need?"

"I make pretty good money right now, but I just want to be able to pay my bills and fix up this place and buy things for my child. Make me an offer."

He did. She accepted. Three days a week at a fair wage. Continued "counseling" every day at 5 o'clock. One kiss per day, maybe with occasional bonuses. He figured a kiss was a good way to break himself in to the world of sexuality and would give him some much needed time to work through the hurdles the Church might put in front of his leaving the priesthood.

    She said, "Let's go out to dinner. Do you like barbeque?"
"I love it," he said. And she grabbed the keys to her Pontiac.

Fresh Paint

    Over the next few weeks, Arjana moved his things into Andret's apartment. Art supplies. Clothes. A drawer-full of miscellaneous stuff. The pan that Andret touched when he made their first eggs together. He donated the rest to the thrift shop. Monifa needed the couch-bed, chair and kitchen table for now. She could get rid of them when she moved her own things in. First, she wanted to paint the whole place.

    All three of them decided to make painting day a festive occasion, symbolic of all of their new lives. They selected a bunch of music CD's to energize their redecorating work and started in with gusto. The living-bedroom became pink with touches of lime green trim. The kitchen saw itself become corn yellow. Monifa painted the table violet. She was just not in the mood for "dull." The tie-dyed scarf she had thrown over the chair the other night had inspired her.

    The bathroom became a deep rose with black and white tile. "Oh, I am feeling better with every color!" she remarked. Arjana presented her with one of his paintings, "Moment of Majesty." It was perfect on the bathroom wall.

    As he hung it over the tub, he reminisced about the time Andret had bathed him there, such a turning point for his life.

    Then, he got back to work. "Maybe Monifa will have a turning point here too," he thought. Maybe this child will really turn her life around. It did seem to usually take another person's energy to help someone make a big shift. He had Andret. He had seen the spark ignite in several of his friends when they met the right person. And all of the new people he was meeting seemed to imply that their partner was a major influence on the up-leveling of their lives. So, this could be it. Of course, he had not yet heard about Father Thomas.

    "I've been meaning to tell you guys, I am going to work

starting next week down at the church. Father Thomas gave me a job doing secretarial work. We are doing counseling together."

"Congratulations!" Arjana and Andret replied in unison. "Who is this Father Thomas? Is he cute?" they teased.

"Mmmhmm," she said.

"Be careful," said Arjana. Grandmother just told us that there is a wave of love hitting the planet and we should be on the lookout for situations in which we might have to make a difficult decision about the appropriateness of our behavior."

"Too late," she said. "We agreed to limit ourselves to one kiss a day."

"Oh no," said Arjana. "You're kidding, I hope."

Monifa started to whistle and kept on painting.

"Look, Monifa," said Arjana. "You can't move here and start your old lifestyle, and with a priest no less. Please."

"Mind your own business, I say. It's not what you think. I actually like the guy. He seems very nice and wants to help me."

"But, you are beautiful," said Andret. "You are very beautiful."

"Thank you." Monifa appreciated the compliment. She had been lucky, she guessed. Men were almost always attracted to her. It was a blessing and a curse. She really did not want to hurt Father Thomas. But he did say that he was leaving the priesthood. Maybe she should ask him more about this plan.

"He's leaving the priesthood," she said. "It's going to be okay."

They continued to paint, not knowing exactly where to take the conversation from here. Arjana began to make silent prayers that some almighty force would keep her in line or at least slow her down so that she could make wise choices. But, working with the guy... that was pushing it. Andret pondered the quirks of fate that brought him to Arjana and now was bringing Monifa into the arms of a priest. How was this going to work out? He hoped for a similar happy ending.

Monifa remembered the golden light that had filled the room the first night she slept here. She wished she could paint that golden color, but pink would have to do. Maybe the golden light would come back of its own accord. After all, it hadn't been invited before. Or had it?

Meeting the Father

"Stick around, you two. Father Thomas is coming over at 5 o'clock. You can meet him then and see what you think."

Exactly at 5, Father Thomas knocked on the door. This time he had a box of chocolate-covered cherries. "I found them," he said. "Enjoy." Then, he noticed the two visitors at the other end of the room. "Oh, I'm sorry, I didn't know you had company." His heart sunk.

"This is my brother, Arjana, and his friend Andret," she introduced them. Father Thomas picked his feelings back up from the floor and said, "So very pleased to meet you, so very pleased." And shook their hands. He banished all the crazy thoughts that said she already had two more lovers. Thank God, that was not true. Thank God.

"Excuse us, we are full of paint," Arjana said. "Monifa is redecorating."

"Can I help at all?" said Father Thomas.

"I think we just about have it under control," said Arjana. They chatted a little more about the colors being cheerful and the snow melting and moving in general.

Monifa said, "I need to change my clothes. Maybe we can take a walk while the paint smell evaporates. You two can go home now. I really appreciate all of your help."

Arjana and Andret got the message and put their tools away. "We'll be back tomorrow about 10 am to finish the trim. See you then. Nice meeting you, Father Thomas." Arjana gave Father Thomas a rather stern, fatherly look, as if to say, "Don't you dare hurt my sister or you will be in very, very big trouble." Then, he smiled and left with Andret.

Monifa came out of the bathroom, looking fresh and ready to go for their walk. Outside, Father Thomas started talking about the neighborhood, how he actually liked the buildings, but the people were not appreciating them enough. He wished that he could raise their awareness, help them to see that it could be so much better. They were all distracted. Wanted to move to a "better" neighborhood instead of fixing up this one. "There is so much potential here," he told Monifa. "Seeing you paint your apartment is an inspiration."

"In the seminary, everything is done within certain guidelines. Divergent interests are not taken into account. Everyone and everything follows the rule. It's a little better being out in the parish, but I look at the city as a whole and think, yes, a city is where shared notions are expressed, all kinds of notions. A city is where they all come together in some serendipitous form. It could be a feast for the eye as well as the soul."

Monifa listened intently as Father Thomas went on to describe what city life could be and all of his efforts to inspire the local parishioners to dig in and create the environment that they would love to be living in. He felt that some understood, but even those usually became distracted by other more pressing problems, work or children or troublesome mates or poverty or just dullness of mind. It disappointed him.

He did what he could at the church. But, it wasn't enough. He wished he had a group of people as inspired and dedicated as himself, but over the years, even he had lost his spunk. "You give me hope again, Monifa."

"I love this talk," she responded. "You actually love something besides a person, don't you? I mean, you love something bigger than yourself. I don't know many people like you. In fact, maybe only Arjana. He always loved something so much bigger. I couldn't see it, but he would try to help me see beyond my immediate environment. Now, I can have both of you working on me," she laughed.

Back at the Victorian, he came in for the kiss. The kiss of the day. The sweet kiss of some amazing new segment of his life. The kiss that allowed love to come to rest in him. Then, he said goodnight and walked home.

Letters to the Pope

As EC traversed her occasional route in the city to find supplies that would benefit the Little People and the Faer Folk over the winter, she came across a couple of very nice red heart-shaped candy boxes. "These would make excellent trays for festive occasions," she thought. Down the block at the church, she often found flowers left over from weddings or funerals. If they were still good, she kind of liked them on her winter table setting even though the Faer Folk frowned on any living thing pulled from the ground in its prime.

Instead, this evening she found a large pile of letters addressed to the Pope. The stationery was of a high quality, and it appeared as though someone was really trying to find the right words to express something, but was having a very hard time. Paper with words was something she was especially fond of, having learned to cut and paste them up to communicate her own thoughts to others. She would have to ask George who this Pope was and why someone would want to write so many letters to him.

These things were about all she could fit into her basket especially before it became too dark to see in the alleys. George would be coming along soon after his usual eavesdropping on the music being played at some of the bars. He never went inside, saying that there were often too many mean spirits there. He would just listen from outside near the stage door. Then, he would find EC and they would stroll home to the woods together.

All of the alley creatures knew and loved EC and George. Cats enjoyed playing with them. Occasionally, Racoon came along with them on evenings when it felt safe. There were often Guardian Angels and Spirit Guides who hovered near the nightlife area of the town, just in case someone suddenly felt bad enough to break out of their resistance to the idea of spiritual beings to call out for help. EC always felt good knowing they were on duty.

The buildings themselves, including the street lights and the sewer grates and the garbage cans and the benches and the umbrella tables all co-operated in presenting the reality that the street walkers, the bar-goers, the police, the homeless people, the lovers, the theatre attendees, and all the other students-of-life had unconsciously agreed upon. It was a magnificent feat of cooperation. EC and George often talked about it on their way home.

The four monks, maintaining their invisibility while downtown, enjoyed following the flow of love as it drifted through the air, in and out of hearts and minds, passing through bodies, opening doors, curling around glasses being lifted in toasts, resting on words being spoken, echoing back through other hearts, other minds and on and on around town.

They took careful note of what was happening to their own initiates as they followed them here and there, paying attention to decisions being made, actions taken and, when appropriate, gently guiding the proceedings. They were not to interfere with the human decision-making process, but could respond to calls for help or, when noting a tricky situation ahead for their charge, they could subtly point to the most spiritually beneficial response.

They were very pleased with Andret's response to the injured Arjana that night in the alley. Recently, Arjana had requested that they be on call for his sister, Monifa, in case she got the urge to resume her bad habit of going out late at night to find some new excitement of a sexual nature. But, they had not seen her. They were, however, pleased with Arjana's love for Monifa and his deepening commitment to Andret. It seemed to them that, indeed, the right place for the Temple of Love had been chosen.

Final Draft

    Father Thomas finished what he perceived to be his final draft of the letter to the Pope. It had to go through other channels, but the official document had to be in his own hand. He felt at this point that he had expressed himself well without negating any of the blessings he felt the church had given him in his years of service. With a great sigh of relief, he folded the letter and placed it in the envelope with a prayer. "Please, dear Father, let this go through quickly and easily if it be Thy will."

    He felt a little shaky afterwards, and decided to walk over to Monifa's even though it was late. They had had their 5 o'clock meetings most days since they became acquainted with each other, keeping to their promise of one kiss per day and usually just going for a walk and talking about life or fantasizing life in the city in its perfected form.

    He put on his overcoat and boots, turned off the lights, closed the door, closing the door forever on his priesthood. He would, of course, carry out his duties for quite awhile longer while his letter traveled through all the channels to the Pope, but that was now a mere formality. His heart and mind had shifted to life with Monifa. "Life with ..." he was unsure if "with" was the proper word. "Life next to ..." "Life alongside of ..." "Life with the possibility of ..." Time would tell.

    At the door of the Victorian, he knocked and waited. The lights came on. She appeared in her bathrobe. "Well, surprise, surprise! To what do I owe the honor of this occasion?" Monifa said playfully.

    "I wrote the letter," he said.

    "What letter?" she responded

    "The letter to the Pope resigning from the priesthood. I asked for release from my vows."

    "Now, that would include the vow of celibacy, would it not?" she asked with a broadening smile.

    "I'm sorry, I didn't to mean to imply that I came here for

... I mean ..."

"Who do you think you are kidding?" She said, half-joking. Come on in out of the cold."

"So, you really did it?" she inquired.

"Yes. I am just feeling a bit shaky. It is as if I have thrown out all of my foundation. I will lose everything. My house, my livelihood ... but my soul is free or will soon be free. I came, I guess, to be reassured that ... well, that you will stand by me during this change ... and maybe longer," he stuttered.

Monifa became more serious now that she realized he was in a serious emotional shift. This was, perhaps, even bigger than when she decided to quit her job, leave her boyfriend, move to Bloomington and have a baby. She at least had Arjana. Who did Father ... should she still call him "father" ... have? "Yes, if you can stand by me during my pregnancy, I can stand by you during your release from the cloth."

They hugged in a deep friendship way while Thomas shed a few tears of relief. She said, "It is going to be alright. I'm going to make us some tea while you just relax a minute." And she left the room. It was then that he noticed the colors of the room in a new way. He had seen the finished project and commented on it days before, but it all seemed more golden tonight. She came back with the tea.

"Here, drink this. Arjana says its the best herb for quieting confusion or distress."

He drank. The love wave had secretly entered through the kitchen door and sunken into the teapot at the invitation of Monifa and all of the kitchen appliances. The other rooms could feel the energy shift and were rooting for the tea to become truly saturated with the love. They all knew that things had been improving for Monifa, but this seemed to them like a key moment that could definitely affect everyone's well-being for a long time to come.

The monks arrived on cue as always, being able to travel instantaneously if needed. Though they did not yet have a personal relationship with either Monifa or Father Thomas, they had the freedom to request permission to observe from the personal Guides of the two. Permission granted.

"I am feeling some extra energy in the room," said Monifa as she looked around curiously. "Arjana has spoken to me of these invisible beings that come around. They can appear and disappear, but they are always helpful, he says. So...." she said in a louder voice, "if you guys are around, we could use some help here. We want to do the right thing. You know more about the situation than we do, so take over." That was all they needed.

Monifa and Thomas both breathed a deep sigh. "The tea really helped calm me," said Thomas.

"I don't think that was it," said Monifa.

They stared at each other for a few minutes, or maybe it was five seconds. The bonus kiss came to their minds and was soon operational. It was perhaps the longest one they had shared thus far. The light in the room became even more golden. It seemed that every single item around them was whispering commandingly, "Yes!" What else could they do ...?

"Thomas," she said, just to hear how the word sounded by itself, without the Father attached to it. He took that as an invitation and began to reach beneath the robe. "Beneath the robe." The phrase stuck in his mind. That was what was happening, he thought. "I am discovering life beneath the robe, the black robe of priesthood, the robe of rules, the robe which has covered my physical body, my sexuality, my explorations of life for all these years."

Monifa expertly guided the proceedings, Thomas being new at such endeavors. It felt very different to her, however, than all of the other men she had experienced. There was something very sweet and innocent about the whole situation. At first, she wasn't sure if she liked it this way, but she wanted his first sexual encounter to be one he would never forget, and that began to inspire her creativity. Yes, she could get behind this idea. Give Father Thomas an experience to write home about ... or maybe to write the

Pope about.

Pretty soon, all those thoughts left her mind and she was just there. Here. Present. Now. And enjoying it fully. When she opened her eyes again, the room was gold; I mean GOLD! She breathed this golden light into herself and something which could only be called "prayers" began to flow from her mouth. It wasn't the Our Father or the Hail Mary. It was more like "Oh My God, Father. Oh, Mother Mary! Let this man be the father of my child."

Father Thomas, upon hearing these words, saw the image of the Heavenly Host, just as he had seen that day in church when he was holding the host up to the heavens and his whole life had entered into it. This time, that life was flowing down from it and into the body of Monifa, into her very womb, into that new life form already growing inside of her. "I am the Father," he said without thinking.

Bryn was now embodied.

The Entrance

     Every structure benefits from an intriguing entrance. How else would you invite the spirit of a place into the building you are planning? Father Thomas was en-tranced by Monifa's opening to him. Monifa was fascinated by the thought of another whole human being having entered unexpectedly and taken form within her very own body. Bryn's soul was given the opportunity to enter into union with these two souls willing to engage in life with him. The entrance to the Temple of Love is everywhere we open to it.

     Hartford was busy designing a physical structure which he hoped would be as enticing as the entrance into human form, a threshold to the sacred realm. Wren was working hard to come up with a landscape plan which would sensually entice visitors toward the partially hidden temple site. Strong arching trees at the beginning providing a sense of shelter and safety. Large, rugged flat stones on the surface of the path for texture and endurance. Bowing grasses. A spread of violets beneath the morning sunrise. A visioning bench overlooking the river. Fragrance from night bloomers and a splash of colors in the distance.

     Nola sketched ideas for the communal kitchen. A larger cob oven would be built on the patio. French doors opening to the summer sun. Sturdy appliances that would last a long time. Clay tiles on the floor. A somewhat rustic but refined feel. Plenty of room for several people to be cooking and cleaning at once. A low counter so that the children could participate in the baking and making of foods. Chairs of various heights. Warmth and easy care were her guidelines.

     Shae imagined the community room with a large open space for dancing and meditation. It needed tall windows with an expansive view. Saffi looked into the details of doorknobs and light fixtures, drawer handles and curtain rods which all had to have a special feel in keeping with the spirit of the place. Keara counseled Wren on the most fragrant flower species and other ways to please the senses. Ayotunde instructed everyone in the requirements of good acoustics and suggested the best sound equipment. Stefan continued to sketch images that would become sculptures in limestone on the facade. Each week, everyone would meet at Grandmother Tsura's to share their ideas, meditate, and relate how the wave of love was affecting their lives.

Father Thomas and Monifa continued their walks around the city. Thomas, now more inspired than ever, enthusiastically explained how the city could become more child-friendly. Bike paths and park-like areas, dotted with businesses that welcome children, small shops that were locally owned and operated by people intending to stay, people wanting to be known for their good works or good products by their own neighbors.

He explained to Monifa that with sufficient resting places here and there a person could easily walk many blocks, shopping and enjoying stops at a bench or a cafe, without any need for a car. Parking lots at the edge of the city could be overseen by nearby business offices or government buildings from which buses would leave to take people downtown. The small river under the town could be unearthed and reclaimed as a design element around which people could gather and lounge on the grass in front of the storefronts and restaurants and stages for musicians to play.

He showed her the beginnings of community gardens and cooperative schools and trails linking city to countryside already in the works. She was impressed. It excited Monifa to think that her child might get to grow up in a sane city where the primary focus was the welfare of all. She could almost feel the child inside her getting excited as well.

As the days went by, Monifa felt more and more that the title "Father" fit Thomas perfectly. Priest or not, he had such fatherly energy. He wanted to care for everyone, to provide what they needed like she imagined a good father would. When he said, "I am the Father," it struck her as truth. Their friendship deepened more each day. She suggested he ease off on the chocolate gifts and learn how to make some healthful foods that would be good for baby and mother both. He was giving it a try. She didn't mind doing the dishes. She just didn't like to cook.

Arjana suggested they meet Nola, an experienced baker, and soon have a potluck with the whole crew. "As long as we have physical bodies," Andret said, "we should nourish them well. They are the temples of our souls."

"This temple thing," said Monifa, "what is it all about?"

"Over the years, maybe going back as far as forty years, Grandmother says, people have been called either by Guides or just by intuition to come to the Bloomington area. Back in the late 1960's, they were responding to a spiritual template called 'World Peace.' By the 1980's, it evolved into a plan called the 'Healing Center.' All sorts of people imagined that they needed to build one and do healing work on themselves and others. They did a lot of learning of ancient and modern healing techniques. This has now evolved into the template with the code name 'The Temple of Love.'"

"Four monks have appeared to us, sometimes in person, other times in meditation, and suggested that we now begin to build the actual physical temple. They informed us that we had already created the etheric stones from which it can be built. These were shaped by our humanitarian actions thus far. I think we still have quite a ways to go in terms of creating enough 'stones' for a temple, but they have instructed us to begin. Make the blueprints. They have agreed upon the land we call the Hill as the proper site.

"One of our favorite children named Bryn has been buried there in an area Grandmother calls 'The Heart of the Beloved.' The Hill overlooks the river Shemaya. Have you been there yet?"

"No," said Monifa, "but I really would like to go. Would you mind if Thomas came along?"

"That would be fine. When shall we schedule the trip?" asked Andret.

"Tomorrow?"

"Tomorrow it is."

A Fluttering

Stepping out of the car, Monifa felt a strange sensation. Her uterus was expanding and whoever was inside there seemed to do a sudden somersault. "Whoa," she said and held her tummy.

"You okay?" asked Thomas.

"Yes, I just felt a real kick this time. There really is a living being inside me and I'm not in charge here."

Thomas took her arm and they walked up the hill with Andret and Arjana.

They went first to The Heart of the Beloved in order to pay their respects to Bryn. Standing at the gravesite, Monifa felt an intense connection to the ground and all that surrounded it. She was a bit puzzled about the feeling, but curious and wanted to spend a few more minutes there. She said, "You all go away for a little bit, I just want to stand here and take this all in. I'm fine, I just feel the need for a few minutes alone."

They were glad to oblige and said, "We will be just over there at the edge of the cliff, come on over when you are ready."

She stood for awhile, then sat down on the ground. Visually, the clearing was just that, a clearing in the woods. But, something inside her ... the baby? ... wanted to touch the ground. She lay down. Instantly, she felt a deep comfort on the spot. It was as if she was merging with the ground itself. She wondered who this Bryn person was. What was he like? He must have been awfully nice for everyone to love him so much. She wanted her baby to be loved as much.

She prayed, "God in heaven or wherever you are, please look at me now. I have a new life inside me. You have also given me a father, a very good father, for my child. I am just asking you to help us make a decent life for this baby so that he can be loved like this boy, Bryn. I think that's it for today. Thank you, Father."

She had never prayed much before, but Thomas was

teaching her the basics. He was careful not to get too preachy about it. But, he was actually more self-conscious about this than she was. She liked his religious talk. It was refreshing. And he seemed to like her plain, straightforward language (except when she went over the top with swear words... that happening less and less now).

She walked over to the edge of the cliff to be with Thomas and her brother, Arjana, whom she respected more each day. She loved Andret, too. He had lifted Arjana to new heights, she thought. She was very grateful. And she got to be in the updraft of that energy, swept away and carried to new heights herself. She was tempted to let herself be really happy.

"Nice river!" she remarked as she put her arm around Thomas.

"Very nice," he said. "Without a car, I have only been here a couple of times and that was years ago. I had forgotten just how beautiful it is here."

They all just rested at the crest. Waves of love passed from one tree to another up and down the river's edge, splashing over the stones, embracing the fish, swirling the weeds, offering drink to the animals as they came and went. It swooped up the hillside, covered the people, laid them gently down in the sun. Sometimes on a winter day, spring actually peeks through. This was one of those moments.

The Laughter of Children

Sounds of young voices came echoing up the path. The grown-ups came out of their reverie and looked around to see Nimi and Carlos coming up the hill. They greeted the young ones and invited them to sit awhile and take in the river view. They introduced them to Father Thomas and Monifa. "This is my sister who has moved here from Illinois," said Arjana.

Under the "how do you do's" Nimi perceived a familiar energy in the vicinity of Monifa's belly. "I know its Bryn," she said to herself. "Oh, Bryn, you have come back, right to our favorite spot." She wanted to run over to Monifa and hug her intensely, to hug Bryn and to tell everyone he has returned. But she held back. Instead, she began to question Monifa. "Will you be living here then?"

"Yes, I am living at Arjana's apartment, the Victorian, in town."

"May I visit you?" Nimi asked.

"Why sure," said Monifa, wondering why this young girl would want to visit her. "I'm open to company. I need to make some friends in the area."

"I'll be your friend," said Nimi. "Oh, thank goodness," she thought. "Thank goodness." And she sent Bryn an intensely focused ray of love.

Monifa felt the love fill up her insides. "Whew," she said, "I'm feeling a little faint, must be morning sickness or something."

"Would you like to go home?" asked Thomas.

"No, let's just walk around a bit. So nice to meet you Nimi and Carlos. I'm sure we will meet again," said Monifa.

The grown-ups continued on their journey through the park, eventually heading home. Carlos and Nimi sat on the Hill together staring out over the river. Finally, Carlos said, "Nimi, something was going on there, what was it?"

"I don't want to talk about it just yet, Carlos. Do you

mind?"

"I guess not," he said. They sat longer in silence ... except that their minds were racing with thoughts. Carlos and Nimi had known each other for many years through their parents' friendship and their years of home schooling. Mostly, they had played children's games together, sometimes studied, worked on a project or attended community events with their parents.

But now that Carlos was feeling his entry into manhood, Nimi looked a little different to him. He had always liked her, but now he had additional feelings that seemed to want to fly out from his body into hers. He really didn't understand exactly what was going on though he had been thoroughly instructed by his elders as to the likelihood of such events. Until it happens, you just don't know. He was beginning to know.

Nimi, however, was oblivious to the whole process. She hardly paid any conscious attention to her body because she was busy attending to the spiritual realms. With Bryn, she was with a kindred soul who also mainly paid attention to the spiritual realms. Carlos had invited her to come to the Hill today, and she never wanted to pass up a chance to be where she might encounter Bryn. Today, he was present!

As you can see, their minds were in two different places. So, when Carlos made a very slight gesture of affection toward Nimi, she recoiled, not out of disgust, just out of total surprise. But, he did not understand. He felt instantly dismissed, dismayed and discombobulated. "Don't you like me, Nimi?" he asked.

Nimi quickly regained her composure, felt sad that she had offended Carlos, and said, "Oh Carlos, I'm sorry. You just surprised me. I didn't know what you were doing. Maybe you could talk to me a little about what you are feeling."

Carlos began to explain how he had recently become a man, how the ceremony had awakened him to this stronger, more mature self, how childhood had evolved into some weird new state that he was just getting used to. He even went as far as explaining the sexual feelings he had begun to have and how he liked to touch himself and what that felt like and that men said that he would really enjoy doing it with a girl at some point in time. How they cautioned him about doing it too soon. How they suggested slow, easy ways to lead up to it without surprising or offending the girl. How being friends was really important. Stuff like that.

Nimi listened with great fascination. She confessed that she had been informed of a few of these things, but figured they would happen much later in life. Not today. She herself had never pleasured herself in the way that Carlos was describing. Had never even thought of it. Did not even know that girls could do such things. But did think that it sounded delightful. Maybe she would try tonight and then they could talk again and compare notes.

This excited Carlos way beyond his expectations, embarrassingly so. He looked at the grass. "Nimi, could I just hold your hand as a friend?" he asked.

"Okay," Nimi responded. And they held hands and gazed again at the river. Nimi was thinking of Bryn, wondering if Bryn had ever touched himself in these ways that Carlos had explained. Wondered if she could experience the physical pleasures that Carlos was enjoying. Wondered about the new baby. Kept wondering.

Carlos, holding Nimi's hand, was wondering what it might feel like if Nimi's hand were touching other parts of himself. Carlos was going into overdrive.

"Let's go home, Nimi. How about if we come back tomorrow or meet somewhere else?"

"Okay," said Nimi. They got up, went to their bicycles, peddled on home. Said, "Good-bye."

Explorations in the Night

At home, Nimi summoned Mama Kate-Amee, "I would like you to tell me everything about sex," she said.

Somewhat surprised, Kate-Amee said, "Sure, let me finish putting this laundry in the machine and I'll meet you in your room. Kate-Amee knew that Nimi had just been with Carlos all day and had a few moments of concern, but then fell back into her basic trust of Nimi's sensibility. She centered herself and went upstairs.

"So, Nimi, what's going on? Has something happened to prompt this question?"

"Well, I was talking to Carlos today and he was telling me of the things boys can do to experience pleasure in their body. He said girls could do the same. Is that really true?"

"Yes, in a manner of speaking, Nimi. Do you have other questions along with this one? I would just like to get the whole picture before I start explaining things."

"Okay. I think he might want to be my boyfriend or at least that he would like to touch me in places that no one has ever touched before. Is that normal? Would I like that? He said I could do it myself and see if it felt good first. Is that true?"

Kate-Amee took a deep breath. "Yes, here's the deal." Kate-Amee explained the anatomy of a woman compared to a man and where the most pleasurable areas are likely to be found in both people. She said that it was beneficial to explore oneself in this regard before letting someone else explore your body. "Sex is best when you feel very attracted to someone, a super-strong energy in their direction. Sex is a powerful, vital, creative energy that should not be given away lightly. It is so powerful that it can create an entire new life. That life will grow in your womb, not anyone else's womb. It will become a baby, and a baby is something you are responsible to take care of for a good many years, like maybe twenty.

"There are birth control methods that can be used to prevent pregnancy, but you are pretty young to be using them. I will be glad to talk to you on that subject when you are ready to actually engage in sexual relations with someone. Right now, I would suggest that you just touch yourself in those sensitive areas to see if your body is ready to experience your pleasures yet. It may not be. Or, this may be the beginning, only you can tell. There is no certain age when this starts happening for everyone.

"I would really like it if you would experiment a little with yourself by yourself, then talk to me again. We can get to more details after you have a little experience. How does that sound to you?" asked Kate-Amee, hoping she had explained enough on the how-to aspect.

"As for what to do with Carlos. He is a very nice boy. I am sure he would like to please you. He is probably feeling his manhood very strongly right now. It is all new to him too, so he will probably make a few mistakes. I mean, he will fumble around, not knowing what to say, not knowing exactly what might make you happy or scare you away. I am sure he would not want to scare you. So, be kind to him. Be thoughtful.

"Once you have a feeling for how your body responds to touches, you will know how to share some pleasures with him. For now, considering how young you are and considering that you have no birth control barriers to pregnancy, I suggest that you not allow his penis inside your vagina. Kissing, hugging, touching ... these things are normal when you feel right about them in your heart, when it is something you want and not just something he wants. Get the picture?

Nimi thought she was getting the picture. "Mama, I think I feel the kind of things you are talking about with Bryn, not with Carlos."

"But Bryn is gone, Nimi."

"No, Mama, he is back. He is living inside Monifa's belly, her womb I mean. I felt him there today when I met her on the Hill.

Kate-Amee was a bit taken aback. "Really? Tell me about that. What was your experience?"

"I just felt this powerful presence in her womb that was so

very, very familiar. I knew it was Bryn. Plus, it was at the portal on the Hill. That is where I would go with Bryn and we would enter the Great Land. He promised he would come back to me sometime. And he has."

"Oh my," said Kate-Amee, and she hugged Nimi close to her. "Nimi, you love Bryn so much. I am sorry that he had to leave this life so early. If he has returned though, he will just be a baby. You would have to wait many years before you could feel that he was your equal again. I am a little sad about this, but we can think more about how it could work out that you might have another relationship with him. It just might not be able to be an adult-to-adult kind of relationship. Do you understand?"

"I think so, Mama."

"This complicates things a little in terms of Carlos. If Carlos comes to love you as a man, then he will want you to love him too. If would not be fair to him if you are still in love with Bryn unless we have found some other way for you to express that love. Let's think and meditate about this for a few days. Do you mind if I talk this over with Papa?"

"I don't mind, Mama. Thank you."

In bed, Nimi rolled into the moonbeam, the place she felt she was most in contact with Bryn. She prayed, "Bryn, thank you for returning. I'm going to find a way to love you here in this life again. You will see. Meanwhile, I have to do some growing up. And, I guess, so do you. Goodnight my friend."

Across town upstairs in the light of that same moon, Carlos imagined Nimi telling him about how she had learned to pleasure herself and asking him to try his hand at the same places. He touched his own body, loving it, fearing it, praising it, being amazed at its power and ability to do such wondrous new things.

The moonbeams had watched lovers come into their own for centuries and were not the least bit surprised or worried about these activities. Moon knew everything there was to know about sexuality. Understood all the ins and outs of every kind of sexual adventure. Moon knew exactly how to encourage romantic interludes between just about every kind of people in the entire world. It loved this work. Moon often asked the assistance of other planets and stars. Sometimes even called upon the ocean, mountains and plains to help her seduce the lovers into copulation. She dressed them in silvery light, showing off their very best features to each other. Night participated fully in helping them focus on just their two selves, blocking out awareness of just about everything else.

The night, the moonlight, the sound of water flowing, the song of nature's creatures in the background. Who could resist? "Hardly anyone" was the answer. Moon saw to it that her young friends freshly discovering their sexual energies would be guided by everyone and everything around them. She seldom made mistakes. Maybe never.

Sure, things could get complicated, but this was mostly human doing. Not the fault of the moon or the night or the bodies of the people involved. So many humans piled so many restrictions and fears on sexuality that they caused unnecessary disasters daily. But Moon was tireless in overcoming these things. Lovers through the centuries have always been determined to overcome any obstacles in their way. Such a powerful force, this sexuality. Such an amazing spiritual force. Moon could see how it might frighten the faint of heart.

With these thoughts, Moon laid her head back on the shoulder of Night and fell asleep.

Lesson Plan

By morning Nimi had decided that she was not really ready yet to do any kind of sexual activity. She just wanted to go over to Monifa's and feel Bryn's energy again. She informed Kate-Amee of her choice and said, "I do want you to tell me more about sex with boys, Mama, but I have other things on my mind right now."

Kate-Amee enjoyed Nimi's serious nature and was somewhat relieved that she was not yet interested in sex. Kate-Amee figured this was a wake-up call, however, and would alert the group that their children were reaching a plateau that everyone should be aware of. It is sometimes hard for parents to shift from thinking of their children as babies to realizing that they have entered a period of having to face adult situations.

The women met at Grandmother's to talk. Nimi was the oldest girl of the group's children, but Mirela was more worldly and would be coming of age soon as well. Aron, Dayo and Nickolas would be following along quickly now that Carlos had entered into his adolescent maturity phase. It was time to review everyone's perspective on sexuality.

"We have done fairly well keeping the children involved in the larger community and yet protected from much of the harshness of the world," said Nola, "but now they are going to be participating more and more without our physical presence nearby. We need to do everything we can to maintain a strong core of guidance for them."

"Sex, drugs and smart phones," Saffi said. "Useful, but dangerous. Yaro hears a lot of stories driving the school bus and talking to teachers. Children have access to things it took our grandparents most of their lives to discover."

Shae responded, "We can certainly arrange some training in the area of sexuality. It is important that we don't just forbid the things we are concerned about. Sexuality is just one expression of the creative spiritual force. I think that one reason our children have avoided trouble so far is that we have thoroughly encouraged and supported their creative inclinations. Creativity never lets you down. Keep that energy going at the same time that you validate their spiritual experiences and sexuality will come in third."

Keara added, "Put them all together and you have an unbeatable combination."

"Okay," said Kate-Amee, "let's brainstorm on how we can do that."

Grandmother then led a mediation in which everyone opened themselves to guidance and inspiration on the subject after which many ideas were shared, and an evening called, "Everything I Want My Parents to Know About Sex" was decided upon. The adult men and women would gather with all the children having asked them ahead of time to bring pictures or drawings of anything they thought of as sexual - good, bad, weird, ugly, beautiful, funny or forbidden. This way they would learn something of the attitudes currently held by the children without making erroneous assumptions. It also sounded like it might be fun for the adults to bring some pictures as well, especially pertaining to their own personal sexual experiences.

The men were informed of the plan and everyone got involved the next week in looking for pictures or making drawings. Throughout this process, the adults and children joked with each other oftentimes and occasionally got to answer important questions for the children. It was a an ice-breaker for everyone on a subject that is often treated either too medically, too romantically or too religiously. The parents made sure the children knew that <u>any</u> picture was fair game; no one would be criticized or made fun of. "We look forward to being shocked, laughing, and learning from you" was the message they all agreed to deliver.

Ripening

Nimi cycled over to Monifa's to bring her some cupcakes she had made and begin to weave herself into Monifa's life. "Nimi, how nice of you." said Monifa inviting Nimi into her home. Would you like some milk with those or a cup of coffee?" she asked, wanting Nimi to know she thought of her as an equal.

"Milk," said Nimi. "I made them as healthy as I could with sunflower seeds in them and cherries so that you would feel good while you are pregnant. It's important to be healthy, you know, when you are having a baby," Nimi informed her.

"Yes, I am reading all about that, Nimi. I have a whole pile of good books here, and Thomas is learning to cook some very healthy meals for us. I am feeling very well, but thank you for being concerned. Why don't you tell me a little bit about yourself so that we can get to know each other better."

"I'm interested in making a new world," said Nimi. "I used to have a friend named Bryn and we talked about this all the time. I would like to have another friend to talk about this with," said Nimi.

"Thomas likes to talk about making a better city. I'm afraid I don't know much about how to make a new world, but I know that it is pretty good right here in Bloomington. I would like my baby to live here in this good world."

"Great!" said Nimi with exceptional enthusiasm. "Can we talk about that, about how to make a good world for your baby?"

"Sure," said Monifa, still a little puzzled at this child's intensity. "Maybe we could start by planning the nursery, you know, like where the baby will sleep, get his or her diapers changed, things like that."

"Oh, it's a boy," said Nimi. "I mean, I am pretty sure it is a boy. You only have two rooms here, so maybe a crib with a curtain around it might work. I think he might like to be in the moonlight though. Is there a window where the moon shines in at night?"

"I think that would only be in the kitchen over here. Maybe we could curtain off this one end," Monifa said. "I have to do a little shopping for a crib and some blankets and things. Would you like to be my assistant? I plan to go on Thursday; would you like me to pick you up?"

"Yes, I will draw you a map to my house."

Thursday morning, Monifa drove up in her old Pontiac. Reuban greeted her at the door. "Arjana has spoken so highly of you, Monifa; I am glad to meet you. Nimi is excited about shopping with you. Would you like to join us for dinner when you return? And please invite Thomas as well."

"Thank you," Monifa replied. "That would be delightful." Monifa scoped out the house and land as much as she could while waiting for Nimi to come downstairs. It seemed to be a pleasant house with enough order to make it functional, but not enough to cause any guest to feel that they had to dress or behave in any certain way.

"Arjana is down at the barn right now. I'll ask him if he and Andret would like to join us tonight as well. You two enjoy your day."

The townspeople were preparing for the holidays, stringing lights, ordering turkeys, wondering how to celebrate all the religions and nationalities that now live in the area, looking for bargains on technological paraphernalia, admiring handmade, American-made, and buying Chinese. Songfests were being organized. Stories were being told. Even the homeless and helpless were imagining that something good might possibly happen.

The world so wanted a rebirth. Birth of the Christ Consciousness. Birth of the child within. Return of the Light. The sighting of angels or space ships or a guiding star. Something radiant. Something extraordinary. And, perhaps, this year it really would happen.

Loose Ends

Monifa and Thomas had sipped from the spring bubbling forth from Arjana and Andret's love for each other and the current carried them into the hearts of all of their friends. Each week at the group dinners, Grandmother continued to encourage everyone to tie up any loose ends from their lives within the old paradigm. "If we are to transcend the things that keep us from entering Higher Consciousness, we need to finish old projects, complete emotional interactions that are still hanging us up, and clear the slate for whatever December 21, 2012, might bring.

"We have all been experiencing the love waves ever since the 1960's. That has worked its way through our lives and personalities in a myriad of ways, eventually drawing us together in our current configuration. We are a powerful group. And we have amazing children coming right along behind us. There is so much more we would like to do, I know, but as we move through this energetic shift in a few weeks, we need to have completed as much of our prior karma as possible."

"I feel one major piece of unfinished business," said Thomas. "I would like to tell my parishioners that I am leaving the priesthood and that I am devoting myself to Monifa and our child." Everyone pledged their support of this somewhat daring move. Thomas hoped that enough people in his church would understand so that he could still feel welcome in the neighborhood.

Nola and Hartford had begun to share more of their feelings about possibilities that might occur due to their differences in age and felt they were facing things squarely. Shae and Wren were building their lives together inspired by their love for nature, devoting themselves to bringing forth beauty wherever they could. Kate-Amee and Reuban felt that parenting was at a new plateau with the children now in adolescence. They had succeeded in enjoying a rich family life in the childhood segment and were ready to tackle the challenges of this new period. Keara and Ayotunde had decided not to become pregnant at this time. They wanted to continue to develop their work together on music and sexuality. Setting up the workshop teaching session for the group prompted by Carlos and Nimi's entrance into the awareness of their luminous field of shared sexuality would be their first endeavor at bringing Ayotunde's musical expertise and Keara's skills in facilitating women's empowerment together.

Everyone felt that, other than the now-being-created plans for the physical structure of the Temple of Love, their lives were in order enough so that their primary focus could be on creating the positive future they had been working toward. Saffi and Yaro, as yet uninformed about the new embodiment of Bryn in Monifa's womb, felt that they needed to focus their attention on how to deepen their relationship with Bryn as he continued his ascension. They were still learning how to do this without continuing to hold onto the vision of him as a child.

Andret and Arjana were totally absorbed in creating their present and future life together as artists, feeling as though their meeting sufficiently severed their ties to the past. Monifa found it fairly easy to let go of the life she had been living, thanks to Thomas and all of these welcoming friends. Grandmother Tsura had experienced the completion of the "Healing Center" portion of her life's mission the day that Stefan found her on the Hill. Together, they were now entering a new period of artistic contribution to the physical Temple of Love and continuing to guide people through the incoming waves.

"The image I have been given by the Guides at this time is that of ascending the Hill in our painted gypsy wagons, circling and sharing as we always have. To me, the gypsy wagon is symbolic of the handcrafted care we always give to our lives. The gypsy archetype speaks to me of devoted friends whose commitment to each other and their own way of life gets them through all of the challenges that befall them. Their loyalty to each other always culminates in a community celebration of music, food, dance, and, of course, lovemaking.

We travel through past and future wearing different

costumes for different times, but always recognizing each other through the chalice of love we carry in our hearts. I lift my cup to each of you for I see that the One I love is Everywhere.

"I have been freed from sorrow and travel along the roads of radiance which will lead me to my next assignment. It may be right here with you simply refining what we have begun. Or, I may pass from view. But, I will be with you nevertheless.

"Some of us began our dance to an exalted rhythm quite a few years back. Others are just learning the steps. Life continues. Let us keep caressing each other's lives and celebrate our future children by continuing all of the daily practices which will affirm the Celestial Earth. Our senses bring us continuous joy when we treat all things as God. This is the teaching I most want to leave with you. You have shown me that you have learned. There is nothing more I need."

What Next?

The conversation continued with everyone sharing ideas on what they were hoping for and working toward in the years to come. Over the years, they had clearly seen the power of their thoughts as well as their actions. They had left behind the ways of thinking that bound them to behaviors no longer useful in a world of love. They had ceased to enter the "fight against" anything whatsoever. This had been a major challenge.

Now, the world outside was quickly crumbling. No, it wasn't buildings falling down or planets colliding. It was thoughtforms dissolving to reveal the spacious place in which heartfelt dreams could be set in the stones that structure a world of love. They had done the work that breaks us out of habitual mind. They had listened and followed the sound of the gong to its source.

The Heart Chalices gleamed. The four monks gathered. The Guides readied their boats. Only a few days left until the crossing.

The Announcement

It was nine days before Christmas and Father Thomas had prepared his sermon. He felt strong. In fact, he felt exhilarated. The entire church glowed with candlelight and smelled of cedar. Statues of angels seemed to be smiling a little more than usual. Even Jesus on the cross had an unusual gleam in his eye. Mother Mary stood by on one side of the sanctuary, Saint Joseph on the other. Father Thomas approached the lectern.

"I come to you today in thanksgiving for all of the years we have been together and to announce a new phase of my life. I am asking that you think for a moment of the times we have spent together, troubles we have been through, celebrations we have shared, and the blessings of God which have been given to us. I am asking that you would continue to hold me in the Light of your hearts as I explain my decision.

"God has led me to embrace another form of service, that of husband and householder. I am leaving the priesthood. I am asking your blessings on my marriage to Monifa who joined us this year. If it were within the rules of the church, I would continue my priesthood, sharing with you all that I learn from my life outside the boundaries. But, that is not feasible at this time. My pledge is that I shall continue serving you and this neighborhood in every way I can.

"I have prayed much over this decision. I ask only that you, too, would pray before judging me harshly. Let the true Light of God be born in our hearts this Christmas. Let us continue opening our arms to each other. God bless you, my friends."

There had been a stir and quiet murmurings in the congregation here and there throughout the sermon. However, when Father Thomas looked up at last from his notes, he saw that one by one, the people were standing. It was not time to stand according to the order of service. This was a standing ovation. A silent prayer of support. A sign that all of these people had actually learned something from Father Thomas. They had learned to love.

After the mass, several of the parish elder men came to him and said, "We will not let them take you from us. We are going to write the Pope and say that we still want you to be our priest. It makes no difference to us whether you are married or not, whether you are celibate or not. We value your spiritual teaching. We are going to protest. Perhaps, there is a better word. We are going to command that this be allowed. It is our church. You are our priest."

Father Thomas was shocked, pleased and a little confused, but gave his consent. If they wanted to go up against the Catholic hierarchy, more power to them. He would not hold his breath, but he would continue his priestly role as long as he could. He thanked them profusely and went home to Monifa's.

Monifa was used to confrontational situations in her old life both in her childhood neighborhood and later with bosses and lovers. She felt she could handle a few Catholics. She sat in the front pew during mass and held steady during Thomas's sermon. She was thrilled at the congregation's response. "This wave of love is nothing to laugh at," she thought. After the service she quickly slipped out the side door so that Thomas could answer any and all questions in his own way. She feared she might inadvertently use the wrong words in her excitement.

When Thomas finally arrived home to her apartment, he told her what the elders had suggested. She was amazed. "They do love you, Thomas. They really do." She hugged him thoroughly and danced him into bed.

December 20, 2012

Carlos lay in bed gazing at the ceiling as he often did, pondering the world of feelings that engulfed him. Suddenly, a vision of himself in royal Spanish clothing appeared. "I am Another You," it said. "My appearance comes from a Time when you were very certain of yourself, living fully in your human power. But, it was not a perfect Time. Society then, as now, was making several errors. I prayed to my God that I would be allowed to view a future in which the problems I faced then would be resolved. That is your Time. Though your Time has also made errors, resolution is at hand.

"You and I are merging now. My gift to you is my confidence. Your gift to me shall be the tenderness of your love. These qualities when brought together shall serve us well as one being. I am from a Time when the polarities of male and female were very distinct. As a man, I ruled. That is different now, and you shall be learning soon the luscious joys of balanced sexuality. Take me into your consciousness. I am the Explorer, the Adventurer, the Victorious One and shall always be at your call."

"Awesome!" responded Carlos. And the vision disappeared.

Nimi's Night

Helping Monifa decorate her apartment for Bryn's arrival pleased Nimi, but she had not been able to actually communicate with the Bryn in Monifa's uterus as she had hoped. Nor, could she clearly hear his communication to her. Still, she knew it was him.

"Dear Bryn," she wrote in her nightly journal communication to him. "I know you are near. I just can't seem to hear you. Maybe it is due to the amniotic fluid you are surrounded by. Are you receiving my thoughts? It is almost the Winter Solstice here, nearly Christmas. The grown-ups are expecting a big Earth Change. What do you think?

"I am not feeling like it is the end of the world even though lots of things are coming apart in the society. I am used to that though. Our group of friends have been doing well as always throughout these upsets. The day I met Monifa on the Hill and realized you had returned was very special, as I have told you. That same day, Carlos became outwardly expressive of his desire to be sexual with me. I was taken by surprise.

"I have thought about it very much since then, spoken to Mama who spoke with Papa. They talked with everyone else and came up with a plan to have a sexuality workshop for all of us. I think this is a good idea because there is a lot I don't know. I wanted to let you know so that you could help me to understand how I can love you and also grow up to love others in some way. I'm going to be open to your communication, so please find a way to deliver a message to me. I'm letting Jampa read this now and deliver it to you with hopes of getting a prompt return.

"Much love always, Nimi."

The Consecration

The four monks were very busy polishing the chalices, making sure the gongs were placed correctly, making candles, and participating in the various choirs. However, all love notes are instantly delivered. It is such a big season on Earth. "More hearts seem to be open this year than I ever remember," said Jampa.

"Isn't that what is supposed to be happening?" asked Chewa teasingly.

Kunchen reported, "There are still many people who are not yet ready. I have been working night and day to get their attention. Sometimes, I wish we had permission to whack them over the head with a whisk broom or something. We have put all of the ancient spiritual traditions on their computer network websites. Information from all of the greatest teachers who ever lived is now available to everyone. You would think no one would miss this opportunity to awaken."

"You are such a dreamer, Kunchen," said Kalden. All of the structures are not yet in place. There are buildings to build, cities to revitalize, inventions to be uncovered. Enough people are awakened though that it will all come about in Time."

"I have released all of my doves this year," said Jampa. "They are circling the Earth at this very moment. Love is happening. You will see."

The prayer bell rang. They stopped their housecleaning and entered into evening meditation, joining all whom they had befriended on Earth. So much bliss was stored in their hearts that it was easy to let it overflow into the hearts of all who joined them.

Snow fell like a blanket of happiness, purifying the atmosphere as it glided to the ground. Angelic voices of the Earthly choirs practiced their songs to perfection. The adept fingers of musicians everywhere touched their keys and strings and the holes of flutes, listening, blending their sounds with their love for this time of year. Grandmothers rocked babies, humming.

Available in 2013

Forbidden Graces, Book Three: The Sanctuary Called Sex

Earth Nation Publishing
812-988-0873
www.sacredarts.info

Other works by Carol Bridges

The Medicine Woman Tarot

The Medicine Woman Inner Guidebook

Secrets Stored in Ecstasy

The Medicine Woman's Guide to Being in Business for Yourself

A Soul in Place, Reclaiming Home as Sacred Space

The Code of the Goddess, Sacred Earth Feng Shui Oracle

Carol's art quilts can be seen at
www.carolbridgesartquilts.com

Grandfathers made sure that everything was in order and safe. Thieves could not think of anything worth stealing this night. Gunmen found their ammunition to be out of date. Angry abusers were suddenly stricken with guilt. There was a long line at Father Thomas's confessional.

Miss Burns decided to retire. Dayo finished his cookbook. Aron began to ask Carlos questions about girls. Keara and Ayotunde continued their research on the music of sex. Everyone was enjoying finding pictures for the upcoming workshop.

"Is there ever a moment when the entire world and every creature in it changes all at once?" asked EC. George asked her where she ever got a thought like that.

EC answered, "It just seems that if all humans were ever able to see all of the infinite realms of creation at once, life would be easier for them. They seem to believe only in themselves until they make a huge mistake. Then, they might let the angels in or God or a nature spirit. It has been such a long time since they have seen us except in their cartoons."

"Sometimes the humans see us, sometimes they don't." George said. "We have been here since the beginning of Time. It is human consciousness which blocks out whole portions of reality in order to accomplish some goal they have decided upon. I never did understand it. Until they recognize the limitations they have placed on their sexuality, the creative force of boundless compassion, they are stuck with their troubles.

"All I know is that their goal seems to be shifting again. More and more people are becoming aware of the consciousness in all things. I think another human creation is at hand." said George.

"But will we be the same as we always have been?" asked EC.

"We will be the same." said George. Then he picked up his harmonica and played their favorite tune. EC let it inspire her day.